Jane Lane was born Elaine K Dakers and her first novel was published when she was just seventeen. She adopted the pen-name of Jane Lane to reflect the historical nature of her books, Lane being the maiden name of her grandmother, a descendant of the Herefordshire branch of Lanes who sheltered King Charles II after his defeat at Worcester. A versatile and dynamic author, Jane Lane has written over forty works of fiction, biography, history and children's books.

D1396444

BY THE SAME AUTHOR
ALL PUBLISHED BY HOUSE OF STRATUS

JANE LANE

A State of Mind

HOUSE OF
STRATUS

This edition published in 2001 by House of Stratus, an imprint of Stratus Holdings plc, 24c Old Burlington Street, London, W1X 1RL, UK. Also at: Suite 210, 1270 Avenue of the Americas, New York, NY 10020, USA

www.houseofstratus.com

Typeset, printed and bound by House of Stratus.

A catalogue record for this book is available from the British Library and The Library of Congress

ISBN 0-7551-0842-6

PART ONE

Chapter One

There was a discreet click from somewhere at the back of the crematorium, and the canned music changed from *Twilight Hour* to Handel's *Largo*. The mini-hearse was late.

Clare bit her lip, feeling the onset of hysteria, and stole a look at the black-clad figure of her elder sister who was kneeling (actually kneeling!) besides her in the front pew. What on earth could Linda have imagined she would get out of this farcical, sentimental nonsense except further pain?

A soft swish of wheels came from outside, the shuffle of feet entering the crematorium, and then the custodian's voice, thick with a cold, intoning something as he preceded the coffin up the aisle. Clare regarded the coffin with horror as it was laid upon a sort of bier beyond a row of potted plants immediately in front of her. A dead body lay within that purple-covered box, a body which, at one touch of an atomic pencil, would have disappeared decently into dust if the modern custom had been followed. Instead of which, Linda had to harrow her own nerves and her sister's by this old-fashioned ceremony. Again Clare glanced at her sister, and saw tears creeping down the white cheek.

Her heart softened. Poor, poor Linda. First, to enter into a marriage-contract with a fool who persisted in writing the sort of reactionary stuff which the Ministry of Literature would not publish; then to have their only child, Charles, State-eliminated because he was suffering from one of the new diseases for which at present there was no cure; and now, six months later, to lose George, her husband, by natural death.

The custodian was standing at the head of the coffin now, still mumbling something. Another discreet click, and the box slid towards a pair of doors which had opened in the wall, and disappeared, the door closing somewhat jerkily behind it. The custodian sneezed twice, rustled away in his picturesque gown, opened a door at the back of the crematorium, and stood there waiting to give each of the mourners a limp handshake.

They gathered outside in a kind of cloister about a pile of flowers, each sheaf neatly wrapped in cellophane. In an iron holder was a card bearing the name of the deceased; they peered at it to make sure they were not looking at someone else's flowers. They were like people standing round a street accident, half fascinated, half revolted. No one knew what to say; figures of aunts, cousins, and friends, unfamiliar in black, reluctantly approached Linda, murmured something stilted about "this sad occasion", and sidled away again.

She stood there apparently unconscious of them, so lost-looking that Clare turned her back, unable to bear it. Across an expanse of lawn, a man in an apron was flinging ashes from a jar on to a rose-bed, his lips pursed in a soundless whistle.

"You'll catch cold, darling," said Clare abruptly, putting her arm round her sister's shoulders, hurrying her without ceremony to the waiting car.

(ii)

As soon as they turned the corner into the square, she could hear Dragon's mournful howl; she had been to get a sitter-in for the dog, and that howl seemed the climax to the ordeal of the funeral. But oh the glorious relief of opening her door, the scrabble of Dragon's long toenails on the parquet, his yelps of passionate welcome, the sight of the cheerful sitting-room, bright with the artificial sunlight streaming through the windows, and reassuring with its modern furniture and gadgets.

Her irritation reawoke as Linda simply stood there, as she had stood above the pile of flowers, the tears running unchecked. Forcing herself to be gentle, Clare shepherded her to an armchair, and for cheerfulness' sake switched on the fire.

"We both need a drink," she said, "and I'll give you a tranquillizer with yours."

There was no answer, and she had to fight hard with exasperation as she busied herself with bottles and glasses. Damn it all, she thought, we simply mustn't have a row on such a day as this.

There had always been a deep affection between the two sisters, but it was an affection without understanding. Linda had received more of their parents' influence than had Clare; the elder sister was in her late teens when father and mother had been killed in the Last World War. They had been the kind of non-church-going Christians so common before Christianity, found to be inimical to the autonomy of Man, had been officially outlawed. They had taught their children to say simple, non-sectarian prayers, and they had based their conduct of life upon certain vague principles.

And for some reason Clare had never been able to understand, Linda had allowed this foolish upbringing to colour her mature outlook. She was not, of course, a Christian, otherwise she would have been banished to the Hebrides, the reservations allotted to these outlaws, and she had no arguments to advance for her attitude of mild non-progressiveness. It displayed itself only in a certain silence when the new uplift services were televised, and in her avoidance of various common expressions such as, "Oh go to the Hebrides!", which was equivalent to the old, "Oh go to hell!" And of course she had become much worse since her marriage to George Coleworthy.

"Look, pet," said Clare with an effort, "I hate to have to worry you when you're so upset already, but you know, this funeral business was slightly dangerous. Oh I know the State still allows cremation if the next-of-kin applies for it and signs all the forms, but the authorities don't approve, because they're always on the watch against the return of superstition. They'll have filed your name, and they'll keep a careful check on you from now on."

It was like talking to a dummy. Linda simply sat there, staring into space.

"Well what I was going to say, Lin, is that it's Wednesday, and APS's half-hour is due any moment. They'll know that you haven't switched on your own television, but surely they'll understand that you'd be here with me. I know you don't like this programme, but honestly, darling, today of all days we must have it on."

She stepped across to the television set and turned the knob to Network 1. The letters A–P–S dropped gently, one by one, on to the screen, followed by the familiar theme of the programme entitled "State Secrets". A moment afterwards, the Prime Minister, Miss Alice Peake-Smythe, was addressing the nation from her rocking-chair.

When first this programme had been televised, care had been taken to present APS as the average British housewife.

One was quite sure she had lunched off canned soup and a broiler from the deep-freeze. But this had not proved popular. For some strange reason even the most forward-looking demanded a State Figure, a Jones with whom he did not wish to keep up. So some very subtle alterations had been made in the setting, and now at her weekly address in "State Secrets", APS resembled a kind of contemporary Queen Victoria; one smiled at her, but with respect; one felt safe with that pouter pigeon bust, that discreetly mauve hair.

The programme began with a hymn appropriate to the season. APS sang it loudly, beating time in the confident knowledge that all the State's children were singing with her.

> *We plough the fields and scatter*
> *The good seed on the land,*
> *But it is fed and war-haw-tered*
> *By Science's mighty hand...*

As the hymn progressed there were shots of a complicated piece of machinery ploughing and scattering, there was artificial rain, followed by artificial sunlight, and finally a view of biliously green corn sprouting. Then APS began her talk. Since today was the anniversary of the first advent to power of the Anarchist Party, it was natural that she should give a résumé of its achievements.

"Let us look back together," said the voice with its faint Birmingham accent, "to that fateful time immediately after the Nuclear Disaster, or the Last World War as we now have the right to call it. It was the Anarchist Party who, sweeping the polls after that holocaust, caused a new Britain to rise from the ashes, first by leaguing with the two remaining Great Powers, America and the East, to ban war; and then by carrying to its logical conclusion the old

Socialist policy of nationalization. What the Socialists never realized, strange as it may seem to us, was that not only things but persons must be nationalized; that we must become one big family, whose head is the State; and since the State provides for all our needs, we belong to it entirely. The manner in which the State does, in fact, provide for its children, is now plain to all.

"It has nationalized money, thus abolishing both poverty and greed. It holds the purse, and its children have only to come to it with their needs for those to be met; naturally after suitable investigation. It is human, and not a mere machine; it recognizes that some require more than others, that the needs of its children are diverse. On its Boards of Investigation are doctors, psychologists, musicians, men of letters, artists, financiers, sociologists. It is far too wise to adopt the old Communist theory of levelling the whole. Every man, woman, and child in its family is assured of housing, education, clothing, entertainment, income, and so forth, proper to the individual need and merit."

This dear mother of ours, the State, APS continued, already had gone far towards bringing the British Isles (most of which, except for Ireland, had been spared by something unexplainable freak when Europe perished in the Nuclear Disaster) up to the standards of health and prosperity already achieved by the more forward-looking America. With the abolition of private ownership, and the making of patriotism a dirty word, there was no longer any reason for men to fight each other. Unemployment and individual poverty were things of the past; British scientists co-operated with American and Eastern in the effort to control Nature, a struggle which, with the full understanding of nuclear power, must ultimately result in the supremacy of Man.

8

Of course, admitted the Prime Minister, with that sturdy realism for which she was so much admired, there were still set-backs. As though conscious of the life or death consequences of the combat, Nature was hitting out with all its malice, and no one could be more grieved than APS over the odd, unexpected, and unexplained weapons which Nature seemed to have up its sleeve. There were earthquakes in region where these had never occurred before, long defunct volcanoes had suddenly become active, and so on. But the end could not be in doubt. The light of the sun was no longer essential when, by throwing a switch, Man could have artificial sunlight all the year round; compulsory birth-control and State-elimination prevented over-population; compulsory inoculation of infants with one of the new wonder-drugs had done away with the old diseases. Again it was true that a few new ones were puzzling the doctors; but it was only a matter of time before these too would disappear.

With her eyes flashing behind the quaint pince-nez she affected, APS appealed to the new interpretation of the Scriptures; after so many centuries of ignorance and superstition, Man at last had realized the meaning of many dark sayings which now, while retaining their profundity, had become simple and true.

"With artificial insemination we have fulfilled the words, 'He maketh the barren woman to keep house, and to be a joyful mother of children.' By legalizing euthanasia, we have obtained that blessing promised to the merciful, and we can now ask with the poor visionary, Paul, 'O death where is thy sting?' Jesus forgave the sins of ignorance and blindness which lead to disease and want; he discovered the 'kiss of life' by which he raised the dead, as indeed one Hebrew prophet had discovered it before him. He was, in fact, the first Modern, the precursor of the Anarchist Party; he tried to impress on his disciples that what he did they could do, and even greater works. And now at last that promise is being fulfilled. Enlightened Man understands that the Kingdom of God is within him, and that here on earth, by his own efforts, he can have Paradise... "

"You haven't touched your drink." said Clare, switching off while APS was still waving a pudgy hand to her audience. "Take the pill with it, and then you can go to sleep for a few hours. I've made up the spare bed; of course you'll stay here tonight."

Her sister obediently took a sip from her glass, but disregarded the small white pill beside it. Standing by the chimney-shelf, Clare looked down at the figure in the armchair; and immediately the artist in her awoke. If it were not indecent to draw Linda now! It was never possible to believe that she was thirty-nine, and strangely her grief made her look even younger. She had the weird loveliness which sometimes comes with illness; the area of darkness round her eyes made them enormous, and the whiteness of her face was unearthly.

Clare started, as for the first time since the funeral Linda spoke. She said in a small thread of a voice:

"Clare, I'm going to the Hebrides."

(iii)

There was just a fraction of a pause while Clare controlled herself. Then she swallowed half her drink, sat down opposite her sister and took Dragon on her lap. She realized that she must behave as unemotionally as possible; and perhaps be a little cruel in order to be kind.

"Look, darling, you've gone through an awful time, and you're thoroughly upset. Will you, for my sake, take that tranquillizer, and then we'll talk."

"I don't want tranquillizers."

"Then have a cigarette," said Clare, repressing irritation. She put one between her sister's flaccid lips and lit it. "You mustn't mind my saying this, but honestly you did make things worse by that frightful funeral this afternoon. It harrowed everyone – "

"It was such a wash-out," interrupted the small voice unexpectedly. "But it was all I could think of to do, and I hoped it might help George. But it was just silly."

"Linda, how could it possibly help George when he's – he's dead? I know it must be hard to realize that, poppet, but – "

Her sister interrupted again, staring at the fire, holding the cigarette which had gone out, talking to herself.

"That figure of Rest above the doors where the coffin went – but how can you rest when there's nothing left of you? And the custodian like a ham actor mumbling his part and not believing a word he said, and no help anywhere. Nobody and nothing meaning anything."

The sight of that wraith-like face and the eyes blind with pain overwhelmed Clare with tenderness. She came and knelt by her sister's chair, taking the ice-cold hands and fondling them.

"Darling, I know what you need. Tomorrow we'll apply for you to enter a Rehabilitation Centre. You're on the verge of a breakdown, and no wonder, but when you've had a month or two under the experts there, you'll feel quite different."

The huge eyes looked at her from out of their pools of darkness, and there was an odd, disturbing compassion in them.

"Shots and pills and probings into the mind and shock treatment and hypnosis and occupational therapy. That's all our age has got to offer those who mourn. Or if the case gets too bad, State-elimination, just as one puts cats and dogs to sleep when they can't be cured. That's what they did to my Charles."

"But that's mercy, Lin."

"You don't understand. You've never lost anyone really dear to you – yet."

Clare felt for an instant as though a hand had squeezed her heart, making her feel sick. She rose unsteadily and went back to her chair.

"And what do you suggest instead, Linda? One's got to face up to life and accept the fact of death. What have you to put in the place of all the things you've been criticizing?"

There was a long pause. Dragon, nursed like a baby in Clare's arms, his favourite position because of his very long body and little short legs, snored gently; from the square came the soft swish of traffic on the rubberized streets. At last Linda said slowly, again as if to herself:

"When I was a child, before the anti-Brotherhood books were banned, I read a poem, and bits of it have stuck in my mind ever since. It was called *The Hound of Heaven,* and it was about a man who was pursued by – well, God, I suppose, and could never find anything that satisfied him because he wouldn't have God."

"Oh Linda! Darling, you mustn't let yourself be frightened by those old fairy-tales – "

"I'm not frightened. At least, well yes, I suppose I am a little, but not in the way you mean." She quoted softly, thoughtfully:

> *"For though I knew His love that followèd,*
> *   Yet was I sore adread*
> *Lest having Him, I might have naught beside;*
> *Yet if one little casement opened wide,*
> *The gust of His approach would clash it to.*
> *Fear wist not to evade, as Love wist to pursue."*

"Yes, it's very fine verse," said Clare indulgently, "but darling, what an awful god! A hound chasing you; a horrible, jealous cruel bogey who won't let you have anything at all if you won't have him. How anyone in their senses ever worshipped such an ogre – "

Linda interrupted again; and for the first time there was a trace of animation in her look and voice.

"You don't understand. I'm not sure I do myself, only I remember more or less how the poem finished:

> All which I took from thee I did but take
>   Not for thy harms,
> But just that thou might'st seek it in My arms.
>   All which thy child's mistake
> Fancies as lost, I have stored for thee at home;
>   Rise, clasp My hand, and come.

I suppose what it means is that if there is a God, and He made George and Charles and me everyone, then we've got to find them in Him. Unless we try to do that, we'll never find them, not the real them, I mean. And anyway they go; everything goes; but it might be just possible that everything you've loved is – well, 'stored for you at home'."

She's mad, thought Clare, staring at this sister who looked and talked like a stranger. Suddenly she was afraid; madness, if it were pronounced incurable, meant State-elimination. She made a great effort to get through to the Linda she knew.

"Darling, you're just talking dangerous nonsense. You know perfectly well that these things are like Father Christmas, or angels in white nightgowns twanging harps. You're just clinging to them as children cling to toys when they're unhappy, but you've grown out of toys. You know they're just bits of cloth and wire, and that you don't really love them."

Linda sighed, suddenly and sharply.

"I don't really think I could love God, even if He exists, but there isn't anything else, and that's why I've got to find out whether He exists or not. And if He does – "

"Well, and if He does?"

"I don't know," said Linda lamely. "But for a long, long while I've sort of felt Him; I haven't said so; it seemed so stupid; and George didn't, so I couldn't talk to him. It's been like a kind of Presence, *there* all the while, not a comfortable sort of Presence, but real in a way that's more real than tables and chairs, and terribly insistent. And so I've just got to find out; I can't run away any longer."

She rose clumsily, pushed back her hair in a familiar gesture, and looked vaguely round for her hat and coat.

"I must go now. I've got to hand in my cash ration book and my identity card and all my coupons. There'll be lots of forms and things to sign, and you know I was always so stupid about those, so will you come and help me make the application?"

"I simply don't know what you're talking about. What application?"

"Why, to go to the Hebrides. I'm not even sure which office you have to apply at, but it won't be closed yet, and I'd like to go as soon as possible, and there are letters and so on I want to destroy before the State takes back our flat."

The exasperation Clare had been fighting all day boiled over. She sat where she was, and said deliberately:

"You're simply dramatizing yourself. You'll either take that pill and go to bed, or else I shall ring up the Emergency Service and ask them to arrange for you to go to a Rehabilitation Centre right away."

There was no answer. Out of the corner of her eye she saw Linda wearily struggling into her coat.

"Linda, don't be a fool! You've harrowed everyone's nerves enough already. You're going to a – "

"I'm going to the Hebrides. I think I would have gone after they killed Charles, only of course George wouldn't have agreed." A small pause. "Come to the Hebrides with me, Clare."

Clare gave one hysterical spurt of laughter.

"Oh this is too much! You're not content to ruin your own life, but you want to ruin mine. You calmly expect me to give up Michael, my work, my comfort, my happiness – "

"I didn't think you *were* very happy lately." Linda took a step towards her sister, and went on hesitantly: "Clare, I've been worried about you. Suppose – suppose Barbara was cured, and came home, and Michael and you had to part. What would you do?"

"Barbara won't be cured, and even if she were, Michael and I are never going to part," Clare answered, flat and cold.

"Please don't be cross. I love you; I always have and always will. I know I'm tiresome, but don't let's part in estrangement. We'll never see each other again. Please say goodbye."

Old affection and new pity fought in vain with a furious anger, the cause of which Clare did not choose to investigate. Very deliberately she leant across the table and drew the telephone towards her. She noticed with fury that her hands were shaking, and that when she spoke her voice was shrill.

"I'm calling up the Emergency Service. They can collect you here or at your own flat, which you please."

"But they won't do either if I'm applying for a passport to the Hebrides," murmured Linda, gently ironic. "You've just been reminding me how merciful the world is now.

Anyone is free to go to one of the reservations when they've signed the necessary forms. Goodbye, darling, darling Clare. Perhaps, after all, I will find you again some day – 'at home'."

(iv)

Clare sat mechanically stroking Dragon for several minutes after she had heard the outer door close. She was cold despite the heat of the room, and this coldness seemed to be centred in her heart. Dragon, aware that her caresses had become merely automatic, grunted and shifted in her arms.

Her hand was still on the 'phone. She half lifted it from its cradle, then let it fall with a clang. For she realized that what Linda had said was perfectly true. Ever since the outlawing of Christianity, the State had boasted of its own superiority in that it did not persecute. If a few of its children were stupid enough to choose a life without any modern amenities, bereft of all communication with the outside world, exiled for ever from their relations and friends, the State, after receiving back from them the various ration books which alone entitled them to live an ordinary sane life, dropped them on the reservations and left them there. It was in accordance with a world which had succeeded in abolishing war, and would have no kind of corporal punishment, that it chastised such declared enemies only by isolation.

She got up after a while and took Dragon for a short walk on the Common. When she returned to the flat, the soundless clock informed her that it was still only six in the evening. That rather shocking fury shivered in her again, and now, whether she wanted to or not, she recognized its cause. "I didn't think you *were* very happy lately." How preposterously untrue! When she loved and was beloved;

when, but for Linda upsetting all her arrangements by her insistence on having that ghastly funeral, Michael would have been coming to dinner. It was Wednesday, their evening. She had made the sacrifice of this one precious evening out of the seven because she had taken it for granted that Linda, having thoroughly upset herself, would stay here tonight.

And then for Linda to dare to suggest that Michael might leave her and return to his mad wife!

She tore off the wretched black frock she had worn to humour Linda, repaired her make-up, and went into the sitting-room. The artificial sunlight streamed through the windows, and would continue to shine for another five hours yet. What in the world was she going to do with herself for the rest of the evening? Wednesday evenings were dedicated; she was never "at home" on them, so no friends would drop in. A show was out of the question; she would simply worry about Linda all through the performance. Besides, Dragon would howl without a sitter-in. I ought to ring up Linda, she thought; no, I ought not. She's got to learn that I simply won't have this play-acting. I'll ring in the morning, when she's tired of it.

And all the while she knew what she was really thinking: If only I could ring Michael.

An old, dangerous resentment stirred in her, and for once she made no effort to control it. Michael was almost as bad as Linda, with his senseless, hurting obstinacy in standing by a marriage-partner who was in a Mental Home. A waste of two lives, her own and Michael's, this living in different flats: an insult to herself that he would not even let her 'phone him, making her wait till he chose to ring her. "We've got to be careful, darling; if Barbara got to hear about us, it would send her completely round the bend."

Clare poured herself a stiff drink, defiantly. When she drank alone she always became emotional, and she had

had quite enough of emotion for one day. What she ought to do was to work; she was behindhand with her illustrations for this new book, and already had received a polite note from the Ministry of Artistic Development reminding her of the fact. But she could not be expected to work this evening after that ghastly funeral and the row with Linda. So she told herself, trying to silence the voice inside that whispered that this was merely another excuse to avoid the work which, until she met Michael, had been her whole life.

From the age of four she had displayed a talent with brush and pencil amounting to genius, and this, as she grew older, became occupation, recreation, and a sort of religion combined. Her satisfaction when the newly formed Ministry of Artistic Development had recognized her talent by creating her a State Artist, giving her the right to put the letters S A after her name, had been due far more to the fact that henceforth she could devote herself solely to her art, than to the luxury, fame and substantial income such an honour entailed. But of late years another obsession had eclipsed the old one, and her work, though it retained a superficial brilliance, was effortful, even at times hateful to her.

Drinking here alone, her mind began on the familiar treadmill. She would have to have a serious talk with Michael; it was intolerable to expect her to go on like this. She must tell him, gently but firmly, that unless he applied to the Ministry of Divorce and got free from Barbara, their relationship must end. She began to rehearse what she would say; she would make it clear to him that he, who vowed he loved her more than anyone else in the world, was denying her the only thing that could make her happy, and denying it without reason, for a mere whim.

She could point her arguments by referring to George and Linda, those glaring examples of people who let whims rule their lives. George had condemned his wife and son to a low income-group simply because he disliked being told what to write, though he had no arguments worth speaking of to advance against the accepted philosophy of the age. And Linda, clinging to fairy-tales which she herself admitted she did not believe, had got to the stage when she proposed to go to the Hebrides, a threat which, if carried out, would involve her family in the ultimate disgrace of modern times.

But all the while that hateful voice in Clare's mind insisted that she would never say any of these things to Michael, would never have it out with him, because anything in the world was better than estrangement, even though their present harmony was only on the surface.

When Dragon had been taken for his final walk, there were still hours before bedtime. And suddenly she knew how she would fill them. She would kill that hateful seed of doubt, uncovered in her heart by Linda, of holding Michael if a cured Barbara came home. She would kill it by re-reading her journals.

Not the later ones. There were too many quarrels recorded in those. The first six months, the long honeymoon, when it had all been unclouded love and happiness. She got out the thick book, settled down beside the fire, and read the opening scene of that play which was *not* going to turn into a tragedy.

"March 1st... "

Chapter Two

(i)

March 1st, and she awoke in a bad temper. She had to go down to Hastings to see an author whose book she was illustrating, and he was a man she did not like. Moreover she was having difficulty with the illustrations; the scene of the book was winter, a winter dramatic with snow, and for years now there had been no snow. Every winter was the same, nondescript, dingy, bleak, and the artificial sunlight somehow made it worse.

It was before the advent of Dragon, and she had no reason to get up until it was time to catch her train. A curious, new, and disturbing thought struck her as she lay there; for the first time she could remember, she felt out of tune with this streamlined world. Enthusiastic for the new art forms, as for all the ideas of her day, hitherto her inspiration had accommodated itself perfectly to these. But suddenly this morning she did not want to work to order; she wanted to achieve with her pencil what this particular author had achieved with his pen; and not (and this was the disturbing element) to have to concern herself with the book's moral, that Christmas was superstitious and barbaric, and that Man, in the period of the story, had been a prey to the natural elements which at last he was learning to control.

20

This would never do, thought Clare, remembering George, her brother-in-law, and his insistence on writing what he and not the State wanted. She got out of bed, drew back the window curtains; and stood transfixed.

Outside her window was an ornamental cherry, and overnight it appeared to have burst into full flower. The illusion was so real that it was several moments before she could withdraw her gaze from the miracle and see the mundane but still exciting explanation. For the first time for years, there had been a heavy fall of snow.

Gazing at that exquisite world, sparkling under a pale blue sky, lying hushed under that strange silence which snow brings, the air pure and cold, all her ill temper vanished. Here was the snow of childhood, crunchy, glittering, remembered only as a dream; spring was just round the corner, and winter had dressed it like a bride. Every tree, which yesterday had drawn with twiggy pencils so busily across the colourless sky, now wore a powdered wig; those slender twigs were furred with impossibly broad white bands; and here and there, though no wind stirred, there was a little private snowstorm from an overladen bough.

What a day for walking on the Common, thought Clare. The hockey-field would be a white arena cobbled with grass tuffets; the pond would be a grey mirror in an ivory frame. The cedars would spread angelic wings, and the familiar walks, the familiar views, would be new and exciting. But by this evening the snow would have melted, and she would have seen it only from the windows of a train. Well, she must do her best. It was what her mother would have called (without really meaning it) an answer to prayer. Here was the snow she needed as a model for this book; she could photograph it on her memory and make sketches of its effects during the journey to Hastings.

For the first half-hour of the journey she might have been alone in the compartment, so absorbed was she in the fairy countryside sliding past outside the window, and in committing it to her drawing-block. But during the stop at Lewes, she became aware that in the opposite end of the carriage sat three other passengers; and as the train pulled out of the station she even forgot about the snow.

Two children, a boy of about fourteen, and a girl who looked considerably younger, sat side by side; across from them was a man, probably their father. It was the little girl who held Clare's gaze, for all the beauty, all the innocence, and all the solemnity of childhood seemed to be embodied in her. Scarcely knowing what she did, Clare tore off from the block the sketches she had been making, and began rapidly reproducing that loveliness on paper. The child made a perfect model, for she sat absolutely motionless, looking still busy with her pencil; and as the man rose to lift down the luggage from the rack, she glanced at him and saw that he was looking at the sketch.

All through the interview with the author she had come to see, embarrassment amounting to shame nagged at the back of her mind. For now she was aware that she had sensed, even while absorbed in her sketching, that there had been something the matter with those three people.

They had not spoken to one another, and yet there had been no atmosphere of disharmony; rather the reverse. They were like friends united closer than ever by some common tragedy. None of them had read book or paper; the children had neither fidgeted nor looked out of the window. It was true that nowadays children seemed to have lost the spontaneous gaiety of her own childhood, and that the bond between them and their parents was growing steadily weaker, for they were taught to regard the State as their parent, and besides, with the advent of the new terminable marriage-contracts, couples seldom stayed together for more than a few years.

But the solemnity of those two children had had a special quality. They had shared with the man, Clare was sure, some unhappy secret; and she had sat there sketching one of them, doing it for her own ends, intruding into their private lives, marshalling into her service a model who could not defend herself from this unwelcome attention. And the father had seen the sketch.

It was destined to be one of those days when the unexpected becomes the rule. First that astonishing view from her window just when she was needing a snow-scene; and now, on Hastings platform, waiting for a train back to town in the late evening, there was the father standing alone, obviously about to catch the same train.

One of the attractive facets of Clare's character was a natural and endearing shyness which she had retained despite success and even fame. But at the moment her shyness was less than her determination to apologize for her bad manners on the outward journey; and though she realized that the man deliberately chose an empty compartment when the train drew in, she followed him into it. Enclosed with this stranger in the little square box, she said impulsively:

"Do excuse me. Perhaps you won't remember, but I travelled down from London with you this morning, and I – I did something which must have seemed to you in the worst possible taste. I made a sketch of your – of the little girl. You see, I'm an artist. I illustrate books; and – well, the fact is I just got carried away by the beauty of that child. Here's the sketch; please destroy it, and then you'll be sure I can never make use of it commercially."

He had been sitting at the other end of the carriage, drawing on an empty pipe, but now he came and sat down opposite her, smiling faintly as he took the sketch. As he studied it, she studied him, not because she was interested in him as a person, but with the instinct of the artist eternally seeking copy. He was a man in his middle thirties, though the lines on his face made him look older. They were new lines, she thought, engraved by some sort of suffering. His eyes were a curious colour, between green and hazel; the sensuality of his mouth was offset by a very determined line of jaw. A vulnerable man, she decided, but one who had contrived an armour for himself. His voice when he spoke was well-bred and quiet.

"You have the most extraordinary gift, if I may be allowed to say so. It's Janet to the life. May I keep this sketch? I shan't be seeing my daughter for a while, and this is so much better than a photograph."

"How terribly nice of you to take it like that! But this is only a rough sketch; if you really want a portrait of your daughter, I could make you one from this, and I'd love to do it to compensate for my bad manners."

"Please, no. I like it just as it is. But I'd be grateful if you'd sign it. I'd like to write and tell Janet that she was drawn by a real artist."

When Clare handed back the sketch, he read the signature.

" 'Clare Bentley'. Of course I know your name, Miss Bentley. David, my son, used to love your work before he grew out of the children's books stage." He smiled ruefully. "They seem to grow up so terribly quickly nowadays."

"I know. I have a nephew, Charles, about your son's age. I only see him occasionally, and each time he's a completely different person."

There was a pause, and her shyness came over her again. They were only at Lewes now, and she felt that the rest of the journey would be trying for them both, for, remembering his silence on the outward trip, she supposed he did not want to talk, yet was too well-mannered to read, now that a conversation had been started. But, offering her a cigarette, he said with easy friendliness:

"It always seems to me that to question artists and writers about their work is frightful cheek. You don't ask a doctor about his patients. All the same, I must admit I should love to hear how you set about it. It's a foreign world to me."

Clare had suffered much from the impertinent curiosity of strangers, and had resented the inevitable questions – "Do you have to wait for inspiration? Do you draw from life? Do the publishers tell you what to draw? How many hours a day do you work?", and so on. But this man, while sensitive enough to realize how irritating that sort of thing could be, was, she was sure, genuinely interested. He proved an intelligent and sympathetic listener; and by the time Terminus Two was reached she discovered with a shock that she had been talking about herself throughout the entire journey. As though he perceived her sudden embarrassment, and guessed its cause, her travelling companion said:

"You've made a journey I dreaded a very pleasant one. Would you perhaps take pity on me, and have a drink somewhere?"

"Take pity on you?"

"I'm going to miss the children horribly tonight. I feel I shall be able to face the empty flat far better if you can spare me another hour of your company."

He explained no further then. It was only after the drink, which became several drinks followed by dinner, that he told her that Barbara, his wife, had become mentally ill. The doctors pronounced it temporary, but meanwhile, until he could apply to the appropriate Ministry for a housekeeper, he had taken his children down to an aunt in Hastings.

(ii)

Clare shut the journal, and took the whining Dragon out for another walk.

If only we had never met in that train, she thought; then pulled herself up sharply. Everything was going to be all right; it was simply that she was depressed by that hateful funeral, and the upset with Linda. We've been so ecstatically happy, Michael and I; and if only I can overcome his stupid obstinacy about Barbara (as I shall do at last), life will be perfect for us both.

She had known she was in love with Michael Standish long before she even wondered whether he were in love with her. It was the first time, and the experience was so strange and wonderful that it was enough in itself. There had been, indeed, a few passing affaires before this, but they had aroused no particular emotion, and marriage she had been determined to shun because it would interfere with her work. And now, for the first time in her life, that work ceased to be an obsession.

At the beginning she was too deliriously happy to notice that her work receded into the background. Her horizon had narrowed to the next meeting with Michael; her days were spent listening for the telephone, planning what she would wear when next they met, recalling just what he had said at their last meeting. As to the outcome of the experience, she never gave it a thought; she was entirely preoccupied with the present and the immediate future.

It was a month or two after their first encounter in the train when he entered her flat for the first time. They had dined together and he saw her home; she had hoped for this, and indeed had arranged for it, filling the flat with flowers, setting out drinks. He had been very silent during dinner, even more silent than usual, and already she had discovered that he was a listener rather than a talker.

26

She had never asked him much about himself, and he had volunteered very little concerning his personal affairs after that abrupt confidence at the end of their journey from Hastings. She knew that he was employed in one of the Ministries, and was in a good income-group, that he had a flat in Kensington, and, during his wife's detention in a Mental Home, was allowed a State Housekeeper. Of relations other than his children he did not speak, but of these children he would talk readily, especially of Janet whom plainly he adored.

"Won't you come in and see where I live?" she asked, lightly but with her heart in her mouth, "You've often said you'd like to have a look at some of my work."

He hesitated for a second. Then he smiled, and followed her in.

Clare had never found her flat in the least lonely. Indeed, privacy to the extent of isolation was a thing she had always prized, and occasions when social good manners constrained her to entertain acquaintances (for she had no close friends) had been in the nature of tiresome interruptions. But she would have been lonely if Michael had not accepted her invitation; suddenly she knew that she had reached the stage when to love was not enough. From looks and tones and silences, she was pretty sure that her love was returned, but now she must hear him say so.

At the time she thought that the way he did say so was odd; but the mere fact of the confession drove away all speculation about the nature of its oddness.

"I'm dangerously fond of you, Clare."

He was standing in front of the fire, turning and turning a wine-glass in his hand, looking down into its contents. There was a little pulse beating in his cheek, twitching and jumping nervously. As she did not reply at once, he raised his eyes and looked directly at her; and there was some strange appeal in them, something almost desperate.

"I'm dangerously fond of you, Michael," she murmured then, making the adjective playful.

He thumped the glass down on the chimney-shelf, spilling half its contents, and seized her in his arms. There was nothing then, that night, or for many weeks thereafter, but sheer ecstasy, robbing her of thought.

I'll take a strong pill, she decided, giving Dragon his supper, and then I'll go to bed. With any luck I'll dream about those good days. I will not, I positively will not go back to the old treadmill tonight. And when Michael 'phones tomorrow, I won't say any of the things I planned to say after Linda left this evening. I'll just accept the situation, as I've often vowed I will. Anything in the world is better than disharmony.

She repeated this sensible resolve to herself like an incantation as she got into bed. But, sleeping instantly as though stunned (such being the effect of this drug), she was precipitated into one of her worst dreams. She re-lived that horrible black day when she had received her first shock.

It was one o'clock in the morning, and he was dressing to go home. She lay on the bed, her eyes following his every movement; she was excited by a new and wonderful discovery which had come to her during the past few hours like a revelation.

"Michael," she said, "do you know, I love you, Yes, I mean but really. I'm not just in love."

He did not answer, and sitting up on the bed, she laughed.

"How ridiculous we are! Or rather, how inhospitable I am! Of course you must come and live here. Why did we never think of it before?"

She had expected a rapturous response, but there was only silence.

"Michael?"

"No, darling, it can't be done."

The flat decision of his tone made her blink; and a horrible, an intolerable fear pounced on her from nowhere.

"You mean – you don't want to – to make it a permanent thing?"

"I want to be with you for ever and ever, but it's impossible."

"Because of the children? But surely that could be arranged. They're at school most of the time, and you could keep your flat on so that they could come there in the holidays. I mean, until you've arranged things with the Ministry of Divorce. I'm not all that selfish, Michael; naturally you want to have your children – "

"Clare, love, I'm married. One day Barbara will come home and she's the mother of my kids. She'll need them, and she'll need me."

Clare got off the bed and put on her robe. She felt that she had to be doing something; also she was aware of that instinct common in a crisis, the feeling that she would be better able to cope with the emergency if she were dressed.

"Let's go into the sitting-room and have a drink. We've got to talk this out."

He did not want to "talk it out"; she knew it; and her fear grew. More than fear; the first faint stirrings of resentment. She sat down on the hearthrug where he liked to see her, switched on the hearthrug where he liked to see her, switched on the sham fire, lit a cigarette. It was hideous that after so recent an intimacy, after so wonderful a revelation that she loved him apart from his body, she should feel that he was withdrawn from her in spirit.

"Look, Michael, we really must get this situation clear – "

"Yes, my love, we must." He was still terse, but now she realized thankfully that when he said "my love" he meant it. "Clare, I was honest from the beginning; I told you I was married. I'm not in love with Barbara; I'm in love with you, but – "

"Good Brotherhood!" burst out Clare. "You talk like someone in an old novel. 'Marriage', 'married', 'till death us do part', Michael, *darling*, we're living at the end of the twentieth century, not in those barbaric days when marriage was for keeps."

"I took Barbara on," said Michael doggedly. "She's my responsibility, especially since her illness. When she comes out of that Mental Home she's got to find me waiting on the doorstep. Don't you see?"

"No, I don't, You made a mistake; or rather you couldn't possibly foresee that she would go – that she would have this mental trouble, or that you would cease to love her You're just being masochistic, Michael, condemning yourself to misery."

He was standing above her, so that she had to look up at him; there was that about his attitude which made her uneasy, for it had a suggestion of impermanence.

"You take something or somebody on," he said, "and you've got to stick to them."

"You talk like a Christian."

"I'm not that." He smiled wryly. "I know I sound stupid, Clare, but you can't change me. Barbara is going to get well, and she will need me. I can't let her or the children down."

"And what about me?"

"You've got your work."

She rose clumsily. She was trembling from head to foot.

"I see. You were just amusing yourself. I wish I'd known."

"That's not true, darling, and you know it." He put his arms round her, yet with more fierceness that affection. "I love you and I want you. I don't love and I don't want Barbara. But there's such a thing as loyalty."

"Just a word!"

"It isn't to me." He released her, and began to wander up and down. "I can see how silly and out-dated it must appear to you; as you say, I sound like a Christian, but I've never been that, could never be. The trouble is, you're the complete modern; I'm not. There are certain things I'm no more capable of doing than of flying through that window, and to desert Barbara is one of them."

"She may never be cured," murmured Clare, shamelessly seizing on that crumb of comfort.

"She will be. They are sure of it. It's only a question of time."

"But what about me?" she cried again, desperate. "Didn't you 'take me on'?"

"You don't believe in permanent contracts; you've often said so."

"But don't you owe *me* any loyalty?"

He did not answer.

"Well then! Is a contract that was never intended to be binding, more than the love which exists between you and me? Isn't love the only tie?"

"I loved Barbara once."

She winced; she did not want to think of that. She made her first acquaintance with jealousy of the past.

"But you don't now. If you cease to love me, I shan't hold you; never fear that – "

"I know you wouldn't try, and I can't imagine ever ceasing to love you. But you've got to accept me as I am, Clare, or not at all."

It was an ultimatum, brutal in its plainness. The fear of losing him swept away all other emotions then, and like a drowning woman she clung to him, her voice making promises, while her femininity assured her secretly that with patience all would yet be well.

But from that day onwards, the fear that had been sown increased, and with it misunderstanding and jealousy. She was no longer content with his body; she wanted his heart, his whole heart, and it was denied her. She had crashed against a rock, and she could neither remove it nor avoid it. In the warmest tide of happiness it would bruise her; in the calmest sea of contentment she would see it gleaming blackly through the clear water.

(iii)

She awoke from her drugged, nightmare-ridden sleep to hear the telephone ringing, and Dragon barking urgently.

This will be Linda, she thought, as she staggered, half doped still, into the sitting-room, wanting to tell me what a fool she was yesterday, begging me to do this or that. Linda, sentimental, unpractical, incurably romantic, had always seemed more like her younger sister than nearly eight years her senior.

She lifted the 'phone, murmured "Hallo", and instantly stiffened. It was not Linda's, but Michael's voice that had answered, and with an odd breathlessness. She glanced at the clock. It was nine in the morning; he had never rung at such an hour before.

"Hallo, *darling*!" she cried. "Do you know, you got me out of bed. I had the Hebrides of a day yesterday, and took a strong pill. How sweet of you to ring so early; any chance of our meeting today? Even half an hour would cheer me up after that ghastly funeral – "

"Yes, love, I'll be round at ten."

"But that's wonderful!" A pause. He said nothing; and she was conscious of her heart beginning to beat with rather sickening rapidity. "There's nothing wrong, is there, Michael?"

"I can't tell you on the 'phone, my love."

There was a click, and the instrument buzzed against her ear.

Feverish activity descended on her. She must dress, take Dragon out, make the sitting-room tidy. Thank Brotherhood the State Cleaner did not come till the afternoon; as an S A Clare had the privilege of choosing the time for this service, and devoted the mornings to her work. Her hands were clumsy; she was impatient with Dragon; she put on a dress, decided that she looked awful in it, dragged it off, splitting it, put on another, wondered if she would make coffee or whether he would prefer a drink. They drank at very odd hours, she and Michael, especially of late. She swore when she saw that the gin bottle was practically empty; there was no time to go out and get more on her coupons.

And all the while she struggled with mounting panic, whose allies were too much drink last night and a strong tranquillizer on top of it. Odd, she thought, trying to fix her mind on abstract things, how even yet the scientists had not succeeded in eliminating completely the after-effects of these merciful pills.

He was late. She stood at the window watching for him, every now and then dashing to the mirror to see how she looked. Dragon whined round her; Dragon, as always, knew when something was wrong. She snapped at him – "Be quiet!" And then, as he drooped his tail, she caught him up and hugged him passionately. I can't bear any more shocks, she thought, not after yesterday and Linda. (I must ring Linda, by the way.) But if Michael has a shock for me, it will be a happy one; Barbara's madness has been pronounced incurable, and she's to be State-eliminated; that's what it is. I always knew it would end like that; so did

Michael, but he had this stupid thing about standing by her, keeping the home ready for her return. He's really very primitive, like a hero in a cowboy film; one can imagine him making some grandiloquent renunciation, and riding out into the westering sun. Perhaps that's partly why I love him...

She had gone into the kitchen to make preparations for coffee, when she heard that familiar, personal little ping of the bell. And as soon as she had torn the door open and seen him standing there, she knew. She wanted to scream at him:

"Don't tell me!"

But he said at once, without looking at her:

"Barbara's cured. She's coming home next week."

Chapter Three

As the train pulled out of Terminus Three, once called Waterloo, and began to gather speed, Clare was conscious of a childish disappointment.

This was the moment which ought to have been full of drama; it was the beginning of her last journey, and she had expected to experience emotion of some kind, even if it were only a natural nervousness. Instead there remained that utter inertia of mind and body which had been growing on her throughout the past months of strange and tedious formalities necessary before she could obtain permission to take this final step.

I shall never see London again, she reminded herself, trying to awake emotion; I shall never have to wait for a 'phone call which I know won't come, never have to see that horrible white telephone sitting there on the table, mocking me with its silence, never have to rush out into the hall dry-mouthed to sort through letters for one I know won't be there. The end of pain is in sight; I am free.

But it was useless. Her heart remained absolutely numb. It was as though that last meeting with Michael on the day after George Coleworthy's funeral had stunned her permanently, as though the shock of it had killed feeling once and for all... No, not once and for all. If she had believed that she would not be doing what she was doing now. Feeling would return eventually, and she could not face it.

Then she mentally shook herself. This was positively anti-Brotherhood. It was queer how full of unexpected little prejudices and outdated notions one became as the result of shock. The psychiatrist had been really annoyed with her slip of the tongue when she had mentioned the world "suicide"; he had winced as if at an obscenity, as indeed it was. Yet "self-elimination", the term she had used so often and so glibly before she had decided to put it into practice, now appeared to her, in her present mood, pretentious, even faintly dishonest, instead of what it was, the name for a noble and meritorious act.

Trying to be sensible, she decided that the trouble lay in the fact that at thirty-two she was not quite young enough to be free of all traces of the attitudes and what were called morals still prevalent in her childhood. Yet never mind how some obscure corner of her heart regarded self-elimination, it was either that or – well, there was really no alternative, except, she thought with dreary humour, going to the Hebrides. The image of her sister flashed into her mind, of poor, dear Linda, from whom she had heard nothing since the day of George's funeral. That meant that Linda really had gone to the Hebrides, to the community of cranks and outlaws living without artificial sunlight, without mercy-drugs, without even electricity, without the blessing of euthanasia…

Her dull heart lifted a little at that last word, the word which spelled release from incurable pain, whether of mind or body.

She remembered being disturbed, even secretly rather shocked, when, nearly a year previously, the Self-Elimination Act had been passed, removing all restrictions from those above the age of sixteen who wished to take their own lives. (Already, so fast was the pace nowadays, there was agitation for having the age-limit lowered.) But her intelligence had acknowledged both the humanity and the logic of the Act. As long ago as 1961 the Suicide Act had made it no longer a criminal offence for any person to commit, or attempt to commit, suicide; but it had remained not only a social stigma but an offence, punishable by a long term of imprisonment, for anyone to aid or counsel such self-destruction, thus breaking the time-honoured rule that what one may do lawfully, another may help him do.

Ever since the Last World War, Euthanasia had been administered to the incurably sick, to the insane, and to those convicted of more than one murder. The obvious next step was to permit its self-administration to those who, after exhaustive examination by psychologists, were declared by these experts as incapable of facing life in its most civilized form or of fitting themselves into a world which was growing steadily more of a paradise for the forward-looking.

A surprisingly large number of people had taken advantage of the new Act, and the Homes of Rest set up by the State were besieged with applicants. The letters s.e. after the announcement of a death were beginning to occur almost as frequently as the familiar SE (State-eliminated), which of course had long outnumbered the ND (Natural Death). A pathetic little band of reactionaries in Parliament and elsewhere had made a rumpus at the time, gong so far as to accuse the Government of encouraging race-suicide; but the memorable speech in which the Prime Minster had answered that accusation had soon disposed of such nonsense.

It was a speech the nation was not likely to forget, even if it wanted to. Since the beloved voice of APS had broadcast that famous harangue, the most eloquent phrases from it had been framed in every home, inscribed on public buildings and enshrined in the new Brotherhood Anthem.

The State-Elimination Act, APS had reminded the nation, had rid Britain of those old horrors, the hospitals for incurables, the asylums for the insane, Yet there still remained those unfortunate people who, for one reason or another, could not adapt themselves to contemporary life, or who suffered from mental pain beyond the help of the psychologists. Was Man, who at last had learned to be truly merciful, to deny these poor folk the annihilation for which they longed?

"And in choosing such annihilation," APS had cried, her eyes moist with tenderness behind her pince-nez, "far from being selfish or cowardly, they will become our new martyrs. It is necessary now as of old that some shall die that others may live in the fullness of health and happiness. At least until our experts have discovered a remedy for intense mental suffering, the sufferer must be given the right, nay, the encouragement, to remove himself from our midst. We must honour these few; we must applaud them. Painless though their passing will be, their deliberate choice of it, in order that they may not cumber this new Eden of ours with their unhappiness, is still that love which is great enough to lay down its life for its friend. They are the faithful unto death, who, by voluntarily eliminating themselves, shall win for their brothers and sisters a crown of bliss... "

So here was Clare Bentley, alone except for Dragon, in the atomically heated compartment of the automatically driven train, being whirled towards her last home, a candidate for the new martyrdom.

The period laid down by law between an application to self-eliminate and the granting of the petition (no one was going to be able to say that it was carelessly allowed) had been peculiarly exhausting.

A small army of psychologists and psychiatrists had inquired into her case. They noted everything; the merest smile, sigh, hesitation, gesture, all had for them some mysterious significance. All were part of the map of her own psyche, they told her, Her dreams and phantasies, her childhood toys, her preference for a certain colour, her reaction to a particular scent, all were extracted and put down in shorthand. Had she ever longed to torture an unkind nurse? Even such nursery favourites as *Peter Rabbit* and *Alice* typified, it seemed, the conflict between the Static and the Dynamic Ideals.

She became permanently self-conscious, watching herself perpetually. *They* seemed to be vastly enjoying themselves; *she* grew more weary with every day that passed. Even if Michael were free, she could not be happy with him now. Their whole relationship had been pawed over, taken apart, by strangers.

Her chief psychiatrist had begun to wear a patient smile before the end. Never had he known a case with so many unconscious resistances, especially when it came to re-living recent emotional experiences. It was, of course, often the way with the more "civilized" type; but in her case it was abnormal. The death-wish was indeed strong. But he was paid to treat her being, and conscientiously he did his best, carrying out the now time-honoured methods of Dream Interpretation, Free Association and Transference. Day after day in the Analysis Hour they went through the procedure; the dream related; interpolations by the Analyst; further remarks and discussion by the Patient; then the dream taken solemnly to pieces, portion by portion, with everything becoming either a phallic symbol or a sex-repression.

It was over at last. She before the final Board, and someone called the Euthanasia Referee announced that her petition had been granted. He summed up her case. The Pleasure Principle ruled her mental life, making her ego-centric and anti-social. There was nothing to be ashamed of in this; the psychic life of all was made up of impulses aiming at the fulfilment of the Pleasure Principle. She, unfortunately, was unable, even with the help of psychiatry, to modify the more elemental psyche and hold a balance between Feeling and Reason; a defect, the Referee hastened to add, often to be found in great artists. In addition she had, it seemed, a strong Separation Anxiety. In her the psychic conflict was so intense that she was unable to fit herself into civilized society, and this conflict had now reached the stage when progress had ceased and retrogression might be expected to set in.

(ii)

Clare opened her handbag presently, took out the brochure of the Home of Rest for which she was bound, and for the first time studied it carefully.

She had been very grateful, in a dull sort of way, when the new Ministry of Self Elimination had notified her that she was eligible for a Class A Home; not only was her vanity pleased by this admission that her case was especially meritorious, but she shrunk from facing the conditions in the cheaper Homes, and was vaguely disquieted by certain ugly rumours concerning them. Her satisfaction had been complete when, on giving up her cash ration book, her identity card, the key of her flat, and all the rest of the appurtenances of life which now returned to the State which had provided them, she had been informed that a room was reserved for her at Fremley

Manor, near Cranford; for Fremley was acknowledged to be the most luxurious Home of Rest in Britain.

Its brochure seemed to bear this out. It was an expensively produced publication, bearing upon its cover the emblem and motto of the State Euthanasia Laboratories, a dove, and the words *Peace Unlimited*. Its glossy pages contained the sort of photographs and information which used to be found in the tariffs of privately run hotels. There was "A Corner of the Lounge", "The Television Room", "The Turkish Bath", and, on turning another page, something called "The Bar of Happiness". This puzzled her, and for a moment she was annoyed to feel a faint stirring of nausea; could this be the room where the elimination took place?

But obviously no. The picture showed a cocktail lounge, with a counter running across one corner, behind which stood two figures, a man and a woman, in white coats. An imposing assortment of bottles was arrayed on the shelves behind them, and half a dozen little dishes, filled with what appeared to be canapes, reposed upon the counter itself. Seated in comfortable chairs about the room, or perched on stools at the bar, were some of the "guests". Clare studied these closely, hoping to discover from their expression something of the attitude of mind of self-eliminators awaiting what used to be called suicide.

But all she could perceive was something baffling and weird; it was as though each person in the room, except for the two behind the bar, was a replica of the other, for while they were of different sexes, ages, and personal appearance, all wore the same fixed and somehow rather daunting smile.

The remainder of the brochure was composed of a letter welcoming the new "guest" to Fremley Manor. It began, "Dear and noble Friend", and it was signed, "Frederick Reddington, FERS." Mr Reddington was the Custodian of

Fremley, and, as the letters after his name proclaimed, a
fellow of the Euthanasia Research Society (for Science was
still busy perfecting the use of euthanasia in all its forms).
Clare read the letter, and was dismayed by the instant
hostility it invoked in her mind.

It was what Charles, her dead nephew, would have
called "a bleat". It reminded her of certain pious little tracts
she had seen in her childhood, slapping her on the back as
some of the old-fashioned Christians had done, but at the
same time it was thick with flattery. Her name, she was
reminded, would you placed in the local Book of
Remembrance, and read out at the special service ordered
to be held each year on Self-Elimination Day. She was one
with the noble but mistaken heroines of history who had
believed that they sacrificed their lives for the common
good; but whereas they had died by the hand of others,
and for superstitions like patriotism or religion, she, brave
lady, was dying by her own hand and for the happiness of
Mankind.

He was counting the days, concluded Mr Reddington,
until he could receive his new martyr into Fremley Manor,
as she, he was sure, must be yearning for the hour of her
supreme sacrifice which would bring her that peace which
the world, unfortunately, had not been able to give. He
begged to remain hers most sincerely in Brotherhood,
Frederick Reddington, FERS.

Clare was struck by the use of the feminine gender in
print; evidently this expensive place had two brochures,
one for men and another for women.

The train slowed down and glancing at her watch Clare
realized that it must be drawing into Cranford, the station
for Fremley Manor. As she lifted from the rack the suitcase
which contained all the worldly goods allowed her for her
two last weeks on earth, she glanced out of the window. It
was not a part of the country she knew, and she felt a flat

sort of interest in it, for it was one of the Reclaimed Regions.

Previous to the Last World War, Cranford had been one of the new towns, sprawling, hideous, with match-box skyscrapers and glass-walled factories. In the Nuclear Disaster it had been utterly destroyed by the unaccountable effects of blast; and since then, with the population problem solved by birth control and State-elimination, the Government had turned Cranford into what it had been a hundred years before, a country village.

The Ministry of Reclamation had done an amazingly thorough job, making Cranford into a museum piece. National excursions were run regularly to it in the summer, so that the State's children could see with their own eyes how their unfortunate ancestors had lived before the new utopia. There were plastic thatched cottages, synthetic beams, little shops which, while of course run by the Government, masqueraded as genuine village stores; rustics walked about in smocks, pulling their forelocks to the visitor, and there were even earth-closets.

As she stepped down on to the platform, with Dragon in her arms, a man in a grey uniform, with a dove embroidered on his cap, came towards Clare, and with the grave courtesy of some stage butler inquired whether she was Miss Bentley.

"Mr Reddington's compliments, miss," said the man, suddenly producing from behind his back a beautiful bouquet. "He asks you to be so good as to accept this little offering to welcome you to Fremley Manor."

Clare flushed with pleasure, at the same time feeling a twist of her heart. It was more than six months since anyone had given her flowers. (She made haste to stifle a mental picture of so many bunches thrust at her when she had opened the door of her flat to the familiar ring, bunches always ill chosen, for Michael had no artistic sense.) No doubt these flowers had not cost Mr Reddington a penny from his cash ration book; no doubt it was a gesture made to all "guests" of Fremley. Nevertheless her femininity was touched, and her cold heart warmed, by an official welcome which took so graceful a form.

Foolishly she bent to smell the perfect, wax-like blossoms, before remembering that modern flowers had no scent. It was one of Nature's vicious little kicks against her conqueror, Man; the scientists and horticulturists were working busily to overcome this defect in the modern flora, but so far they had not succeeded. After all, one could not have everything at once.

She followed the man towards the booking-hall, through the doorway of which she could see a sleek grey car drawn up. The prospect of companionship, of the distraction of new surroundings and new faces cheered her, and her drawn face lightened in a smile. As she passed through the booking-hall she heard a porter give a soft wolf-whistle of approval and then a voice say:

"Another silly lamb taking itself to the slaughter. Rather 'er than me, mate."

Clare's smile vanished, and a sudden hateful emotion flooded her heart, an emotion she would not recognize as shame.

(iii)

While she was being driven swiftly and soundlessly through the country lanes, the local atomic power stations switched on the artificial sunlight, the actual sun having withdrawn behind clouds as was its bad-tempered habit nowadays. Clare found herself seized by one of her secret, ridiculous prejudices. Oh, it was beautiful in its way, this soft, golden light; but the artist in her detested it because it had robbed the world of the wonder of dusk and dawn, making all things look unnatural, like a picture postcard.

And the sentimentalist in her hated it because, so the scientists thought, it had killed off nearly all the wild animals, that or the artificial sprays and fertilizers now in universal use. (Many of the trees had died too, but this was a minor inconvenience; modern man did not use wood.) Her intelligence, at war with her sentiment, reminded her that in the bad old days wild animals had suffered cruelly at the hands of man, and had preyed on one another. Far better that they should disappear. For all that, she missed the sights and sounds of her childhood, the rustle in the hedgerow, the rabbits feeding in the meadows, the song of a thrush.

The car turned in between wrought-iron gates and drove on through parkland. Here were animals in plenty, sheep and cows, but the sight of these gave Clare no pleasure. By injecting them at birth with the new veterinary preparations, it had become possible to rear flocks and herds of a size and fatness never known before. Indeed, some of the scientists were beginning to be a little disturbed by their size, and particularly by their strength; they were perfectly docile at present, but one never knew. Clare looked at them with distaste, these enormous glossy beasts grazing upon grass unnaturally green under the artificial sunlight.

Then all such idle thoughts were swept away as the car, climbing the last slope of the rubber driveway, purred to a standstill before the main doors of Fremley Manor. Clare's instant impression of her last home was one of keen disappointment. She had always loved beauty, and had hoped to end her life in beautiful surroundings.

Fremley Manor had been built in the era of nineteenth-century industrialism, and even up to the Second World War a single private family had occupied the house. During that catastrophe it had been requisitioned by the Army, and after the war its owners had returned to it, living in one wing and struggling to met taxation and death duties by turning the rest into a sort of museum to which the public were admitted on payment of half-a-crown. General nationalization had put a stop to this deplorable state of things; and Fremley, which had been out of the path of the freak blast in which Cranford had perished, had become first a State School, then, when Cranford was "reclaimed", the local Government offices, and lastly, since the passing of the Self-Elimination Act, a Class A Home of Rest.

It was a blatantly hideous Victorian pile, with an enormous porch like a tent, and, for no apparent reason, a turret sprouting from its roof, capped by a small spire and a weathercock that pointed permanently south. The house had a smugly well-kept appearance, its paintwork spotlessly white, every window-pane gleaming, the door-knocker shining like an artificial sun. On one side bulged a vast conservatory, resembling a growth.

As though her arrival had been watched for, the double doors were flung open from within in dramatic fashion, and a lady appeared at the top of the steps. As Clare came up to her, she clasped the newcomer in a loose embrace.

"My dear, welcome, welcome to Fremley! I am Freda Reddington, and I know we are going to be such good friends. And your sweet little doggie! Was he a booful, was he then?"

Dragon paid no attention to this greeting, but lifted his leg against the doorpost.

"You must be tired after your journey," continued Mrs Reddington, "and tea shall be brought to your room. Afterwards you shall meet our other friends, and if you feel up to it my husband would like a little chat with you."

Prattling brightly, she ushered Clare through a pair of inner doors into a spacious lounge hall, warmed by concealed central heating and also by a blazing log fire, a thing Clare had not seen since her childhood. Everything, she noticed, was as well-kept and opulent within as without. Scentless flowers, most artistically arranged, were everywhere, there were glossy magazines on side tables, bright chintzes on chairs and sofas, a deep-pile carpet on the floor. In fact, Fremley carried out the impression Clare had received of it from its brochure; it was exactly like a first-class hotel.

"If, my dear Clare," chattered Mrs Reddington, taking the new "guest's" arm as they went up a staircase, "– all our friends are called by their first names here, it makes it so much more homely – if you like walking, there are the most beautiful rambles through the park, and you and this little sweetie dachs can wander about to your heart's content. And you must not hesitate to ask for anything you want, anything at all; everything at Fremley is at the service of its honoured guests."

Opening a door, she drew Clare into a large, tastefully furnished bedroom. Old rose curtains hung before the wide windows through which the artificial sunlight streamed, and real roses of a colour exactly matching the curtains, carpet, and bedspread, stood in a vase upon the dressing-table. A deep chair facing the window invited repose; there was a shelf of books, a telephone, a television set, a radiogram, and a silver box containing cigarettes.

"It's a beautiful room," murmured Clare, privately wondering why it should give her the creeps.

"It is our *best* room, my dear," replied Mrs Reddington gently, "reserved for those of our dear martyrs whom we feel to be specially in need of healing beauty. I wish you could have met the dear lady who occupied it before you. She had been some odd kind of a Christian – a Plymouth Rock, was it? – a Plymouth Brother, that was it, or Sister, I suppose, in her case," amended Mrs Reddington with an

47

artless laugh. "She told me that often and often she had wondered whether she might not end it all herself, she was so unhappy, but she could not get rid of the superstitions of her youth. Almost to the end the dirty word 'suicide' kept slipping out in her talk, but I am thankful to say that we convinced her before she went that what she was doing was noble and so right."

Clare murmured something, her eyes straying to the telephone. Surely...

"You have but to lift the receiver," said Mrs Reddington, seeming to read her thoughts, "to ask for anything you need, day or night. There is always someone on duty."

"Oh yes, of course; thank you," mumbled Clare, blinking back foolish tears. She ought to have realized that it was merely a house 'phone; she had cut herself off for ever from the outside world. It must be because she was tired that just for a moment that thought bred a ridiculous kind of panic.

"Ah, here is your tea," said the bright voice of Mrs Reddington, as there came a tap on the door, "Set it down by the window, Mary, where Miss Clare can admire the view. Good girl, you have remembered the bowl of water for our boozie-woozie here; *isn't* he a pet? Would he like something to eat now, dear? No? Then you must tell me when he has his din-dins and what he likes. Many of our guests bring their pets with them; this dear merciful State of ours understands the comfort of our animal friends. We even had a monkey once. There are none at present except for our own rascal, Marmaduke, but we had a cat with a whole family of kittens recently. How they did enjoy 'Purr with Mother' on Network 6! Does this booful like television, eh?"

Dragon yawned rudely in response.

"Now, Clare, I will leave you for an hour to have a rest and freshen up. Your bathroom and toilet are next door, and here is the switch for your electric blanket."

She tiptoed out, closing the door softly behind her, and Clare was left alone with every facility for comfort, and Dragon. Snatching the dog into her arms, she flopped down on the bed, and for the first time for six months she burst into a storm of tears.

(iv)

The tears did not relieve her, and noticing her suitcase, which a porter much have brought up, she went quickly to it and opened it, desperate for the sight and feel of familiar possessions. But as she lifted out her dresses and toilet articles, she remembered that deliberately she had brought nothing of a personal nature with her save these. After Michael had left the flat for the last time on that awful morning she had destroyed everything connected with the Michael-Clare relationship. Allowing herself a last orgy of sentiment, she had burned letters, diaries, souvenirs; what could not be burnt she had parcelled up and flung into the river, making a kind of ceremony of the act.

For there had been the sneaking hope that this destruction of all material reminders of their love would release her from the past and from that love which had become an obsession. But as the days went by, she had realized the futility of such a hope. A very old sentimental song, revived in her girlhood, had kept echoing in her mind:

> *I have taken your picture out of its frame,*
> *And out of my prayers I have taken your name,*
> *But deep in my heart you are there just the same.*

It was true, and she must face it. She *had* faced it, she thought, mechanically hanging her clothes in the built-in wardrobe, and that was why she was eliminating herself. She could not live without Michael, and she could not have Michael because he had done what he had always said he would do; he had chosen to stick by his wife who had returned to him cured.

An overdose of sleeping-pills, taken there and then, would have been the simplest way. But Clare was not lacking in a kind of courage; though she shrank from laying bare the sacred wound in her heart, it was her duty to apply for self-elimination through the proper channels, even though the experts might decide that they could not grant permission. During those horrible months, she had remembered several times what Linda had said on the day of George's funeral.

"Shots and pills and probings into the mind and shock treatment and hypnosis and occupational therapy. That's all our age has got to offer those who mourn."

But oh the infinite relief when she heard the verdict that not all the wonders of modern Science could cure the sickness of her heart. In a year or two, maybe, had murmured the Euthanasia Referee, Man might find a remedy for such an illness, might become indeed the master of his fate. But meantime... She remembered walking away from the Board of Investigation filled with a sudden, blessed peace. She was justified in seeking that for which alone she longed, the annihilation of the desolate, empty, useless creature called Clare Bentley.

The peace had not remained, yet at least there had continued a sort of synthetic variety of it, an almost consistent numbness of the emotions. This she had welcomed and deliberately fostered; such anaesthetizing of her spirit was her only safeguard against the unknown torments which otherwise might assail her during the statutory two weeks in the Home of Rest.

Why two weeks? she wondered, setting out her bottles and jars on the dressing-table. It was a condition laid down in the Self-Elimination Act, but she could not remember, if she had ever heard, the reason for it. It seemed cruel; it was like the time which in the old days had to be spent by a criminal between his condemnation and his execution, a prolonging of the agony. She must ask Mr Reddington to explain. But at any rate here was the ideal environment in which to get through the statutory fortnight.

Here was a strange house, an impersonal room unhaunted by memories. Her companions would be human derelicts like herself, who, for one reason or another, had been unable to find contentment in this earthly paradise... She pulled herself up sharply. Not human derelicts, but martyrs; she really must try to remember that, even though the idea was so novel, and somehow rather distasteful. It was queer how, in this crisis of her life, foolish prejudices she did not know she possessed suddenly began to plague her, how the sneaking thought recurred that the disintegration of her being was somehow her own fault, and not the incurable disease the experts had insisted that it was, that if she could have found out the way she could have cured herself, become again that which she had been before she met Michael, a useful member of society.

And deeper still the fantastic suspicion that self-elimination was not noble but craven. (And there were others who thought that way too, simple folk who, despite years of State Education, retained the old prejudices. "Another silly lamb taking itself to the slaughter." That was how the porter at Cranford station had described her.)

She was putting her shoes away in the wardrobe, when she noticed a scrap of paper lying under the rail in one corner. She stared at it in foolish surprise; in this exquisitely tidy and impersonal room it struck an odd note, a human note; and hardly knowing what she did she fished it out. It seemed to be a bit of a torn-up letter, but no "guest" at Fremley received any communication from the outside world. She took the fragment to the window, and in the strong sunlight made out four words written in a very shaky hand:

"Dear God, forgive me… "

Chapter Four

"Could I – I mean, am I allowed some pills to make me sleep at night?" asked Clare, trying hard to control the trembling of her voice. "I had to give up my coupons for them, you see."

Frederick Reddington, FERS, smiled kindly.

"My dear, very few things, you will find, are *not* allowed at Fremley Manor. Of course you shall have a tranquillizer, but you will excuse me if I do not give it to you until you are ready to retire to rest. For I believe you will find, by the time you have met our friends in the Bar of Happiness, and had dinner and perhaps a game of bridge, that you will sleep naturally. And that is so much better."

He smiled again, bracing, cosy, paternal. He was a thin wiry man, shorter than herself, with a pink polished skin which seemed to exude wholesomeness of mind and body. Indeed the expression, "bursting with good health", perfectly applied to him. Both in appearance and manner he combined the family doctor and the courteous host; he wore a bow-tie, a dark suit, a shirt with the discreetest stripe in it; his speech was very faintly pedantic. He had received Clare in this comfortable, rather old-fashioned room with a warmth which appeared perfectly genuine. The room itself was soothing; it bore not the faintest resemblance to an office or a consulting-room; it was restful with deep leather chairs in place of the modern tubular ones; thankfully Clare noted the absence of works on Psychoanalysis.

Seated on one side of the log fire, nursing the sleeping Dragon, she was furiously aware that on the one hand she was nervous, and that on the other, while instinctively disliking Mr Reddington, she found his manner extremely reassuring, even though she sensed patronage beneath his old-world courtesy.

"We have very few rules at Fremley Manor," continued that gentleman, his capable hands clasping the bosses of his chair, "and those are designed solely for the comfort and convenience of our honoured guests. One of these rules is that at half-past six each evening we all forgather in our Bar of Happiness, and there we chat together and take a convivial glass."

She smiled. The phrase was so quaint and outdated.

"I was never much of a drinking man myself, Clare, but in the bad old days of my youth I always found that despite their obvious dangers there was nowhere to be found so friendly an atmosphere as in the privately run 'pubs', as they called them. You won't remember them, perhaps, but they really were public houses; that is to say that anybody above the age of – er – eighteen, I think it was, could enter and order what he pleased to drink, provided, of course, that he had the money to pay for it. In general the system was bad, yet there was, as I say, that congenial atmosphere of good fellowship which, I must confess, for some reason or other seems to be lacking in our new State Hostelries, fine and well-ordered though they are, where only those who have alcohol-coupons are allowed to enter. That is why, when I was appointed Custodian of Fremley, I instituted our Bar of Happiness, where *all* may enter. I have found it has done wonders in fostering that friendly atmosphere which it is my ambition to maintain at Fremley Manor."

"It seems a most pleasant idea," murmured Clare, feeling that perhaps she would have to revise her opinion of Mr Reddington. "Do you mean it is a real bar, where one can drink without coupons, and there are cocktails and so on?"

"That is precisely what I mean. There are many of our guests, of course, who do not care for alcohol; for these soft drinks of all varieties are provided. Which reminds me; my wife tells me that you scarcely touched your tea. Was it not to your liking?"

"Oh yes, thank you. I – I was just rather upset – "

"Of course, of course, my dear child, I understand perfectly. The first few hours are always difficult for our brave ones, and for those who, like yourself, are sensitive, they can be almost intolerable." He glanced at an old grandfather clock which tick-tocked somnolently in a corner. "We have a little time before our Bar of Happiness opens; would you care for a quiet glass with me here? Now do say yes, for I will tell you a little secret; I could do with a snifter myself!"

Smiling roguishly, he bounced out of his chair without waiting for her reply, and went with his vigorous step to a cabinet which stood against one wall. Throwing open the doors he exposed a gleaming array of bottles and glasses.

"Sherry? Gin and tonic? A dry Martini? Whisky and soda? Ah, whisky! We had a Scotsman here once, who asked for what he called a glass and a pint. How we laughed together when I poured him a pint of whisky, and he had to explain that in his youth the expression had meant a large whisky and a pint of beer! I have made it a trifle strong," he continued, almost winking at Clare as he set the drink down on the little table at her side, "for I believe that you need it. My dear Clare, I drink to you, not only to welcome you to Fremley manor, but to applaud your heroic courage."

The solemnity with which he had spoken the last words grated on Clare, and she was about to make some kind of demur, when Mr Reddington forestalled her.

"Now I am going to be firm. Not a word, please, until you have emptied that glass, and not even then if you do not feel like talking. We have plenty of time for little chats. I am a stranger to you; you are under a great strain, and have not yet entered into the peace of Fremley. You are (I can see it) reserved by nature; your face in proud, beautifully proud; it may well be that you are not disposed to unburden your heart to another. I shall respect your silence; but if and when you wish to talk, I beg you to believe that I am your friend, anxious only for your welfare, desiring only to serve you. If I may use a simile from the bad old days," added Mr Reddington, with an apologetic smile, "I am like a priest in the confessional; all that is told me here in this room is sacred and will never be disclosed."

She had half emptied her glass while he was talking, and now put it down on the table at her elbow. Either it was a very strong whisky, or else Mr Reddington's voice was mesmeric; at all events she felt peculiar, not drowsy, on the contrary very wide-awake, but as though she had been given a drug which, while numbing that raw wound in her heart, left her mind extraordinarily clear and composed. But she was not going to talk about herself, even to so sympathetic a listener; she had had quite enough of that sort of talk with psychologists during the past months.

"There's a question I'd like to ask you," she said, watching the thin blue smoke from her cigarette wavering up into the air. "What is the reason for the law making it compulsory to spend two weeks in a Home of Rest before – before self-elimination?"

"An interesting question. But first, my dear Clare, pray finish that drink and let me refill your glass – no, I insist. You are feeling a trifle relaxed already; I can tell it. A second little tot will work wonders."

Having brought the replenished glass, Mr Reddington sat down again, and placed his finger-tips together in an attitude almost suggesting prayer.

"Now here," he said reverently, "you have a supreme example of the benevolence of our modern world, or rather I should say of our dear Prime Minister, for it was APS herself who caused this condition to be incorporated in the Self-Elimination Act. Our martyrs, Clare, have endured the most painful suffering, sometimes years of it, before they have reached their great decision. Since they, by voluntarily laying down their lives, prevent their unhappiness from disturbing their more fortunate fellow men, it is but just, said APS, that the State should reward them by giving them a little space of time in which they may find a measure of peace and serenity. According to the merits of each particular case, they are given the conditions which bring these blessings, and make them ready for the supreme sacrifice."

"By these conditions, I suppose you mean the maximum of comfort and beautiful surroundings," remarked Clare, a shade of contempt in her tone. "I had those before I came here, but they brought me neither relief nor serenity. I don't see – "

She broke off. Was it her imagination, or had there been a flicker of something vaguely unpleasant in Mr Reddington's eyes as she spoke? But he sounded absolutely sincere as he replied:

"My dear Clare, you will find that it is not only comfort and beautiful surroundings we offer you at Fremley. I shall not particularize at present; and indeed I hope that after a few days with us you will discover for yourself the benefit of our treatment."

Then suddenly, with a complete change of tone and subject, he asked:

"Do you admire that little drawing on the wall?"

She looked at it. It seemed vaguely familiar, but she could get up no interest, and said politely that she thought it very pretty. He gave her a tender smile.

"It's your own work. Yes, an early Clare Bentley. The design on the cover of your first – or was it your second? – children's book. I persuaded your publishers to sell me the sketch. You see, I have always been a fan of yours, my dear Clare; and if I may say so I was a little sad when I heard that our country must lose your exquisite art. And yet how I admire you for your courage and realism in recognizing that you can no longer produce such delightful work!"

"Some virtue went out of me," she murmured, staring at the framed sketch. "It was like turning on a tap and nothing flows."

"And nothing can ever flow out of that tap again, Clare," said the soft, hypnotic voice. "Our scientists have discovered, as doubtless you know, that creative work such as yours in some way depends upon a mysterious thing which used to be called inspiration, and which springs from the heart or the emotions. In ten years' time, please Brotherhood, they will have found the means for making the heart subject to all-conquering Man, as they have made the head; but now, alas, it still defies us. And being no longer able to express yourself, or to contribute to the happiness of your fellow citizens, you have chosen the great sacrifice; you have faced the truth that you can never produce creative work again. Some weaker folk would have gone on turning the dried-up tap; but not you!"

He paused; then, as Clare said nothing, he quoted with feeling:

> "*Bravest at the last,*
> *She levelled at our purposes, and, being royal,*
> *Took her own way.*

The poet Shakespeare. Yes, denuded of the foolish superstitions of his age, his work remains extraordinarily deep in the understanding of human life and its problems. Royal in spirit, you take your own way, the way of self-elimination. You will not, as the coward will, continue to exist as a half-being, distressing all who knew you as you once were, unable to enter into the full and healthy life which Man has achieved for himself in these our days, or to labour for the common good. Finding that there is no cure for your mortal sickness of heart, you will embrace voluntarily, you who are in the prime of life, that which still holds a measure of terror for us all."

"Terror?" She turned the word over in her mind, placidly sipping her whisky. "I don't see how death can hold any terror when there is no pain, when we have nothing left in life to cling to, and when all we long for is complete annihilation."

He smiled gravely.

"Self-preservation, my dear Clare, still remains one of the strongest instincts in man. To overcome it, as you have, is the supreme act of courage." He glanced at the clock, and rose. "Come, my dear friend, it is time for our family gathering. Whenever you wish, we will talk together; I am at the service of our guests at all hours. And I have not forgotten the tranquillizer," he added, placing his hand beneath her arm in a gesture which was fatherly without being offensively familiar, "though I still hope and believe that you will not need it."

(ii)

Certainly they must have been very stiff whiskies, thought Clare, as Mr Reddington shepherded her down the hall, for while she felt none of that dreary sort of intoxication she had experienced during the time immediately following her parting with Michael, when she had taken to drinking alone, she was conscious of a queer and not at all unpleasant lightness of body and relaxation of mind. Deep down inside her there lurked, she knew, the pain she dreaded, like a wild beast in its cage ready to spring; but the cage seemed securely barred at present, so securely that she could almost forget that its inhabitant was there. Though by nature shy with strangers, she felt perfectly at her ease as Mr Reddington, still with a hand beneath her arm, led her through the open doorway of the Bar of Happiness.

It was the picture in the brochure come to life. There were the white-coated man and woman behind the counter, the appetizing little dishes of canapes, the cheerful array of bottles, the "guests" sitting or standing about the room. The curtains had been drawn across the tall windows, and here as elsewhere at Fremley, the homeliness was enhanced by a real fire. She noticed that most of the women were wearing jewellery, and remembered that in a Class A Home of Rest such trinkets were permitted, whereas in the more modest Homes there had to be returned to the State before a "guest" entered. There was a soft hum of talk; two men were playing chess; a woman, who sat by herself, was placidly knitting. In fact the atmosphere was precisely that of an ordinary cocktail bar in an expensive hotel.

No, not quite precisely. She noticed instantly, and with a faint return of the uneasiness she had experienced while studying the brochure on her journey, that upon the face of every "guest" was the same expression, a gentle, dreamy, rather unnatural smile.

"My dear friends," said Mr Reddington, beaming round upon the company, "this is our Clare, an especially honoured guest. I know how welcome you will make her, a welcome you will extend, I have no doubt," he went on playfully, "to her charming little companion, whose name is Dragon. (*Isn't* he a charmer?) As you are tired, dear Clare, I will not make introductions all round, but now let me see, here is a comfortable chair, and here are John and Alison. Stephen, a whisky and soda, please, for Clare. Excuse me, my dear, while I make my little round."

He bowed, and began moving slowly from table to table, pausing for some genial talk at each, while the man he had addressed as Stephen brought Clare her drink. It was fantastic, bizarre, thought Clare, hearing the clink of glasses, the popping of corks, the shaking of cocktails; it could have been a hideous mockery, an orgy of despair, and yet it was not. It was merely strange. It was as though this was already a company of ghosts.

"Such a kind, kind man," murmured an old voice beside her. "He is like a very wonderful faith-healer I went to in my young days. Of course there is no such thing as faith-healing; I know that now; but Mr Edmundson really did make me feel better because he was so kind and understanding, just as Mr Reddington is."

Clare observed the speaker. She was a very old lady, frail and shrunken. She sat holding hands with John, obviously her husband, and a masculine edition of herself. A couple from the long past when marriage was considered indissoluble, a perfect Darby and Joan, with a lifetime of affection behind them. Automatically and yet tenderly the old man handed his wife his cocktail cherry, then produced a clean handkerchief to wipe her fingers; he bent down to make sure that her feet, in their tiny, old-lady shoes, were comfortably set upon the footstool; he nodded his head and smiled fondly whenever she spoke.

What in the world, wondered Clare, are such people doing here?

"Such exquisite dry sherry," continued Alison, taking bird-like sips from her glass, "and to think that it is given to us free! And such beautifully cooked food, as you will see presently at dinner, my dear. I really think that the Right Honourable Alice Peake-Smythe must be what we used to call a saint."

Clare blinked, unable to follow the purport of this remark.

"My dear wife," said John, in his dry old vice, "is very deaf, and so I fear you will not be able to carry on a conversation with her. But I do so agree with her, Miss Clare. You must forgive me, but I find it so difficult to get into this habit of addressing strangers by their Christian – oh, I do beg your pardon! – by their first names, without any sort of prefix. I entirely agree with my dear wife, as I was saying, that APS, as she is familiarly called, is a very wonderful woman. What my wife meant, of course, was that it was APS herself who suggested these two weeks of luxury and comfort; but to me what is so horrible is to think of what would have happened to us before this Self-Elimination Act."

He leaned closer to Clare, and went on, tremblingly confidential:

"My beloved wife is a victim of one of the new diseases for which there is no cure, and was due for – er – State-elimination. But when I appealed to the authorities who deal with such cases, asking permission to – to come to a Home of Rest if my dear wife could accompany me, they at once agreed. After fifty years of marriage, you see, I could not… And so we shall – er – go together."

Clare was conscious of a kind of nausea, mingled with pity.

"You mean you are prepared to eliminate yourself, even though you might go on living quite comfortably?"

He smiled an old, wise smile.

"There would be only half myself if Alison went. But no, I think perhaps I am not being entirely honest. Old age, my dear Miss Clare, is a heavy burden. Oh pray don't misunderstand me," he went on, pathetically earnest. "I know they have done wonders with all these new drugs, keeping people alive long after what used to be called the natural span, but one still gets so tired. I remember when I was young seeing the old being a burden on their relatives, and then, of course, there were the Twilight Homes, but somehow even those didn't answer the problem. They longed to be gone, those old people, but the foolish and cruel belief was current that human life was sacred, even though a man or woman had become blind, or senile, or otherwise a nuisance to themselves and others. Doctors used to take some kind of an oath, I believe, which forbade them to shorten life. It was terrible, terrible," he murmured, shaking his old head.

"Yes, I do agree with you," said Clare, though rather at a loss to understand which era he was speaking about.

"I believe," continued John, "that there is a Bill to be debated by Parliament whereby all persons over a certain age will be State-eliminated, and that will be a very great blessing. One gets so tired," he repeated with an unconscious sigh. "After all, we are just like the animals; you would have found that one day, when he got to be fourteen or so, this dear little dog of yours would have wanted nothing in the world but rest. But there! I am a foolish, sentimental old fellow, my dear Miss Clare, and I must confess that I find a comfort in sacrificing my life voluntarily for the sake of my beloved wife." He patted the old lady's hand, and said loudly and clearly: "Not too tried for our piquet after dinner, I hope? You must give me my revenge, you know."

"With Mr Reddington's compliments," said a brisk voice, making Clare jump.

She looked up and saw the man named Stephen setting down another whisky at her elbow. As she encountered his glance, she experienced a feeling of discomfort, not untinged with hostility. He was looking directly at her from beneath drooping lids, saturnine, enigmatic, quizzical. He did not wear the universal smile she had noticed on the faces of all the other "guests", though she had taken him to be one, and beneath his surface courtesy she sensed something which she did not like.

"Thank you," she said curtly, "but I won't have any more."

He lifted his eyebrows, bowed, and moved away. It was a relief to Clare that at this moment she heard the gong boom out opulently for dinner.

(iii)

In the large and handsome dining-room, with synthetic candles gleaming in wall sconces, and a portrait of APS benevolently regarding the diners from over the fireplace, the inhabitants of Fremley all sat at one enormous table, as though at a banquet. Mr Reddington presided at one end and his wife at the other; and white-jacketed waiters came and went between the table and the serving-hatch with dishes of the most expensive food.

Clare found herself seated in the place of honour at Mr Reddington's right hand, and as the soup was served he explained to her that at Fremley all changed their order of sitting at lunch and dinner, "so that our dear guests may get to know one another". Breakfast, he added, was served to the guests in their rooms, and tea also if they so desired.

"You are wondering, no doubt", he went on, buttering toast with cheerful efficiency, "about the empty place on my left, and why there should be a flower laid upon it. It was the place of one of our dear friends who left us this morning, and it is my custom to honour the memory of our martyrs in this fashion on the day of their departure from us."

Clare stared at the empty chair and at the plate with the hothouse rose laid on it, and her mouth went dry. She was not afraid, but that sense of the bizarre had returned in full force.

"I wish you could have met Edward," continued Mr Reddington, tenderly caressing the rose. "He was only a boy, not yet twenty, but so wise and charming. And in such a pitiable state when he came to us. Even I, who have had so much experience in seeing the change Fremley works in our guests, was touched and astonished by the serenity with which he left us – excuse me", he added, as a waiter bent and whispered in his ear, "I am wanted on the telephone".

Deserted by her host, Clare glanced across the table, and immediately encountered the slightly mocking eyes of the man named Stephen. To distract her attention, she turned to her neighbour, intending to begin some of the ordinary small-talk habitual between strangers; then suddenly realized the grim impossibility of such talk here. With the outside world shut out for ever, with death brooding over them all, what was there to talk about? Did one, as in hospitals, discuss one's case? Certainly she was not going to discuss hers with anybody. With infinite relief she heard her neighbour open the conversation.

She was a very plump lady, this neighbour, with what used to be called ample curves; she looked exactly like an old-fashioned chorus-girl in her decline. Hair of an unnatural corn-colour was piled in two great mounds upon the small head; the little face, which in its youth must have been pretty in a chocolate-box way, was thickly painted, making it mask-like; the buxom figure was clothed in a purple velvet housecoat, rather faded, and the still slender hands were loaded with rings.

"Felicity," murmured the lady. "That is my name, dear." And then, with an odd note of appeal: "Felicity Cummings."

"But – surely I've seen your picture somewhere," said Clare, touched by the note of appeal and desperately searching her memory. "You were a great stage star, weren't you? I'm positive I've – "

The heavily made-up eyes brightened and filled.

"But how wonderful that you should have heard of me! You are so young. Perhaps your mother would have seen me in *Take your Partners,* my greatest success. It was a Royal Command performance in the days of the Monarchy, and it ran for five years and three months. I shook hands with the Queen. Would you like me to show you my press-cuttings and all my lovely souvenirs?"

"I should like it very much," Clare lied kindly.

"Tomorrow after tea. We have a little time to ourselves then, for dear Mr Reddington is always busy with interviews, and it will have to be tomorrow or the next day, because after that I go. Of course you won't know any of the girls and boys in the photographs, but you may have heard of some of them."

"But have you not – not acted lately?" asked Clare, feeling it was something she should not ask, but unable to restrain her curiosity.

The lady glanced at her, seemed about to speak, then curved her mouth into that odd, slightly unnerving smile universal among the "guests" at Fremley.

"I'm sorry," mumbled Clare, abashed. "I shouldn't have asked something which perhaps revives painful memories."

"Oh no, dear," said Felicity, "they're not painful at all and I love to talk of them." She looked round with a furtive air, then, lowering her voice, she burst into confidences. "I have not acted since the theatre was nationalized, and that, as you know, was a long time back. They did not think I would be suitable for the modern plays, and of course they were right. They were perfectly right, darling," she went on earnestly, and yet with the air of one repeating a lesson. "It wasn't that I lost my talent, but I just could not get into the parts I should have had to play. You see, it's all so different now, and really it was beginning to be long before nationalization."

"I'm afraid I don't quite understand."

"There was a different kind of right and wrong, if you see what I mean, and the old kind of right always had to triumph in the end. It must seem so silly to you, but that was the way my generation was brought up. Of course there were the problem plays, as they called them, even in my youth, but mostly the hero and heroine had to live happy ever after." She gave an apologetic little giggle.

Clare laid down her fork with a hand which was not quite steady.

"And that," continued Felicity, playing with the fillet of sole on her plate, "very seldom happened in real life, and so it was wishful-thinking and wrong. But it was nice to pretend, and somehow I couldn't get out of the way of pretending, even though I always knew it was hard on women, particularly the pretty ones. Poor darling Marie-Rosie – did you ever hear of her, I wonder?"

"I – I think so."

"She shot herself, darling; dreadful it was, and all because of that cad of a Rochester. Blood everywhere,

67

darling, and an inquest, and people saying nasty things, using that horrible word 'suicide'. And that night she'd given the greatest performance of her career. I was playing the juvenile lead at the time, and so proud to be in the same show with her. I couldn't believe it when her dresser came screaming on to the stage after the final curtain, saying that Marie-Rosie had shot herself in her dressing-room."

"It must have been a shocking thing. And such a waste of a great talent."

To Clare's surprise, Felicity did not respond with any great enthusiasm to this conventional remark.

"Well yes, darling, of course it was that, I know. But it wasn't her death that killed her, if you see what I mean. She wouldn't have been able to go on acting after Rochester deserted her. An artiste's heart has got to be fed – are you feeling all right, honey? You've suddenly gone so pale."

"Yes, I'm all right," Clare said almost inaudibly.

"It was the waste of herself that seemed to me so terrible, and I still think it was terrible, though of course I shouldn't, for I know now that what she did was noble and right. And so wonderfully brave, doing it all alone like that, knowing people would call her a suicide, and actually pulling the trigger, and all that blood – though of course she wasn't there to see that. But she was always so kind and so *human*, if you know what I mean. My first night in the show I was standing in the wings all of a shiver with nerves; she noticed me – she, such a great star and me a nobody! – and what did she do but send her dresser to fetch me a wrap till I had to go on. And I shall always remember how she put her arm round my shoulders, and she said, Felicity, she said, you're going to be a wow. (That was an expression which was all the rage then.)"

"And so you were."

"And so I was, darling, but that was long afterwards. And I never came near to being such a wow as Marie-Rosie. Or such a great person."

A tear, stained with mascara, fell on her ample bosom, and she laid one ringed had on Clare's arm.

"I know I can trust you, darling," she whispered, "not to breathe a word, for Mr Reddington wouldn't like it, and I know I'm being silly and what they call wicked nowadays. But I still hope that when I go in two days' time I'll meet Marie-Rosie, and all the boys and girls I used to know in the Profession. Oh, I'm not a Christian; you mustn't think that. But somehow I can't get around to thinking that my pals aren't somewhere any longer, and that I won't have a chance to thank Marie-Rosie for being so kind to me when I was a nobody. And I'd like to tell her that what she did wasn't a crime at all, but that she was a great martyr as well as a great artiste. Though somehow," added Felicity, with a tiny sigh, "I don't think she'd care about the martyr part, dear. In fact I think she'd probably use a rude word about it."

"You are not drinking that nice Burgundy, my dear," said the kindly reproachful voice of Mr Reddington, addressing Felicity.

The plump lady, with a guilty start, immediately lifted her glass.

(iv)

"Never mix wine and spirits," said a too familiar voice in Clare's mind. She had a sudden vivid little vignette of Michael saying it, his curious coloured eyes squinting at her as he lit his pipe.

Well, I bloody well mixed them tonight, she retorted, trying to hate him, drifting through the lounges of Fremley, feeling not drunk but odd, very odd indeed. Beer on whisky, always risky; burgundy on whisky – what? She had better find Mr Reddington and ask for that tranquillizer; but no, it was too early. Dragon would need to be taken out again before she went to bed.

An extremely handsome lady named Margaret asked her to make up a hand of bridge with Richard, a middle-aged man with the face of a scholar, and Enid, a little woman whose fluffy white hair standing up on the top of her head, and her large-eyed, pointed face, gave her the look of a poodle. Clare excused herself, and glanced into the Television Room, but the brightly coloured figures on the screen made her wince. *They* were all right; they had adapted themselves to the new nationalized Art. And so had she until she had met Michael. Fell sick of Michael; that was how she thought of it sometimes. He was like a disease in her blood.

By the log fire in the central lounge an elderly woman sat by herself, winding wool from a skein she had draped round the back of a chair. She was the same woman whom Clare had noticed knitting in the Bar of Happiness. Of all the incongruous occupations in a place like this! For whom could one knit? Who would ever wear that half-finished sock lying in the comfortable lap? So far as the outside world is concerned, you are already dead, my dear, Clare wanted to say; and heard herself ask instead:

"Would you like me to hold the wool for you?"

Patient eyes looked up at her.

"That's ever so kind of you! It's years since anyone held my wool for me. Charlie, my husband, always used to, for you see, I never had a daughter, only sons, and you can't expect boys to do a thing like that. Have you got any children? Excuse my asking, for I see you don't wear a ring, but there are so many of these what they call bachelor-mothers about nowadays, who have this artificial insemination, I mean," she added, going a little pink.

"No, I haven't," said Clare, sitting down on a stool and extending the skein between her hands.

The woman reminded her of her own mother, a dim, domesticated person, kindly, efficient in her own sphere, busy with a multitude of petty tasks, much more interested in her family than in the mighty events which had shaken the outside world in her middle age, far more concerned about Linda getting 'flu, or Clare cutting her finger than in the horrors of nuclear warfare or the wonders of the dawn of paradise on earth.

"I can't bear to sit with my hands idle," said the woman, busily winding wool and glancing up at Clare with just a trace of that queer, unnatural smile common to the inmates of Fremley. "(I'm Mrs Smith, by the way; oh, I keep forgetting about first names; mine's Jane.) When you're sixty, you can't, you know, sit idle, I mean, though I know it's very silly. Mr Reddington say I'll get over it; I only came here yesterday."

"I haven't seen anyone knitting for a long time," remarked Clare. "I thought it was all done on machines. It must be hard work, by hand."

"I like hard work," said Mrs Smith simply. "That's really why I'm here; isn't it silly? But it's such fun; I mean it was, when there was someone to work for. It's not being needed any more that I couldn't stand. Somehow I thought a mother would always be needed; wasn't I daft? But now Charlie's dead, and the boys have gone in for these marriage-contracts, and are so modern, which of course is right and proper, and their wives have the knitting done for them on machines, for the grandchildren, I mean, and anyway I can't ever remember which wife is which, for each of the boys has been divorced at least three times – what was I saying?"

"I think – I think it was about liking hard work."

"Oh yes, how silly of me. Charlie always used to say, Janey, he used to say, do try to be lucid. And then he'd come and give me a big hug. Ever such a kind man was my hubby. Yes, well, we both had to work ever so hard, because we were poor and had a big family."

"How dreadful! To be poor, I mean."

The capable hands, with a thick gold wedding-ring half embedded in the flesh of one finger, paused for a second.

"That's what the boys used to say when they grew up. And I never could explain that it wasn't. We was a team, Charlie and me; we used to plan little economies, and we had a china dog on the mantelpiece where we used to put whatever we'd manage to save at the end of the week, and round about November, when I was making my Christmas pudding (you must excuse me, dear, but I just couldn't fancy the ones you bought, though I'm sure they're ever so nice), Charlie used to say to me, That dog's getting fat, Janey; looks like we'll be able to have a leg of pork at Christmas, *and* a bottle of port-type, I shouldn't wonder. And we was always independent; that was a great blessing; never owed a penny; and when the neighbours used to say, Mrs Smith, what on earth do you do with yourselves of an evening, you not having the telly, and never going to the flicks or the bingo-hall? Why, we play cribbage, Charlie and me, I used to tell them, when the children are in bed; or sometimes he sits and reads to me while I do the mending."

There was a pause, while Clare tried to think of something to say. Mrs Smith's case made nonsense to her.

"But surely," she observed at last, "after having had such a hard life, it must have been great not to have to worry over money any longer, to have security, to be kept by the State, to have all your chores done for you by a State Cleaner. It's one of the real blessings of this age that women don't have to slave at housework any longer – "

"You don't understand, dear," mildly interrupted Mrs Smith. "It wasn't slavery if you had someone to work for, someone you loved. It was – well, I suppose it sounds silly, but it was a sort of creating all the time, making things for people, even if it was only a pudding or a pair of socks. And owning things, too, buying them with money you'd earned, and then looking after them, thinking while you was polishing the furniture that your children would have the same things when you was gone. You were a kind of – what's the word? – steward for them, if you see what I mean. But now we don't own anything; it all belongs to the State."

"You sound to me," said Clare, with a shade of contempt, "as if you'd be happier in the Hebrides."

The woman laid down her knitting, and the patient, puzzled eyes looked directly into Clare's.

"I thought of that, I really did. But I wouldn't find Charlie there, because he's dead, and I'm too old to begin another sort of life on my own. But I wish, you know, that when I die I could be put into a grave with him."

"A *grave*?"

"Yes, I know, that must sound horrible to you, because you're young and modern. But it was a comfort. It was a thing I missed dreadfully when my hubby died, not having a place where I could go and put flowers, and know that one day I'd be lying there with him. Morbid, that's me! At least, that's what all these clever doctors, these psycho-what-you-call-'ems thought, when I had to go to them before I came here. Ever so rude they were, dear," went on Mrs Smith, lowering her voice and turning slightly pink again; "told me I'd been in love with my own father when I was a little tot. Well, I mean to say! Oh, I'm sure they're very clever, but they just don't seem to know anything about ordinary people; they don't even think there are any ordinary people. But there are, you know. I'm one."

She counted stitches for a moment, and then went on:

"They gave what I was suffering from ever such a long name, but I could have told them what was wrong with me. It's just that nobody's ever going to need me no more. I thought Tom, my youngest, always would. Oh, I've never interfered once they're married; that wouldn't be right. But I did think that just sometimes he'd want to come and see his old mum, and that perhaps he'd ask me to sew a button on now and again. A terrible one for losing his buttons, was my Tom. Well, never mind. One day's gone already, and it'll all be over in less than a fortnight, and meantime I can pretend I'm knitting these socks for someone, and think about the old days."

Chapter Five

Like a child afraid of the dark, Clare dreaded the night; and for some months now she had not been able completely to escape its horrors by sleeping-pills. She was strongly resistant to drugs, and one pill, powerful though it was, had ceased to be sufficient. Two or three would induce, not genuine sleep, but a void of unconsciousness; she would pass immediately from horrible wide-awakeness into a kind of coma, and waking reluctantly, sick and dizzy, in the morning, was more tired than when she went to bed.

But as she undressed on her first night at Fremley, she felt a blissful drowsiness. She had forgotten to ask Mr Reddington for a tranquillizer, and it was too much trouble to call him up on the house 'phone; besides she felt convinced that for the first time for years she would sleep naturally. Perhaps it was the effect of the fair amount of alcohol she had taken during the evening, though ordinarily alcohol made her emotional, as she had found to her cost when she had taken to drinking after Michael left her.

There was, of course, nightmare to be faced; and, experienced in these attacks of the unconscious, she made her preparations. Like an old soldier she had learnt what measures of defence must be taken against the enemy's night assault; as soon as she woke, sweating and crying from an evil dream, she must switch on the light, put her hand under the eiderdown to feel the comfort of Dragon's soft warm body lying on its back with short legs flaccid in sleep, light a cigarette, and wrench her mind to the solving of a crossword puzzle. They were feeble defences, but the best she had been able to invent.

Having seen that light-switch, cigarettes, a pencil, and a crossword were all within reach of her hand, she opened the window without looking at the night (an autumn night was one of those many things which evoked the image of Michael), and got into bed. Dragon, his long thin tail and short hind-legs protruding from under the covers in an abandoned posture, gave a small protesting grunt.

She slept instantly, a heavy, exhausted sleep, and the inevitable nightmare delayed its attack till it was nearly morning. When it struck, it had no connection with Michael.

She was being pursued by something, what she did not know, nor dared she look back to see. Only there was a conviction in her mind that this Thing did not like the wonderful new inventions of modern man, and that if she could make use of them she could escape it. Her heart thudding, a stitch in her side, she ran doggedly along one of the great motorways, recklessly dodging swift cars that raced at her soundlessly on the rubber roads, shrinking back from their headlights. But still there padded behind her the feet of her pursuer, untiring, effortless, purposeful.

If I can reach an airfield, she thought, I can catch a plane. It can't follow me into the air... Now she was in an aircraft, leaning back in her seat, borne swifter than thought to some unknown destination. But she knew that outside the window the Thing kept pace with the plane, that it would still be there when she landed, that there was no escape...

She was running again; but now the commonest experience of nightmare happened; her feet refused to obey her will; they collapsed from under her, and the shadow of the Thing blotted out of the world. She looked at last at her pursuers, and saw it was her sister Linda. A Linda transfigured, sun-tanned, radiant, with a basket of dark blue berries on her arm, her hands stained with their juice. Linda held out those hands, and cried softly, joyously:

"Oh, it's such *fun*! Come with me, Clare; come home!"

"There is no such place as home!" cried Clare; and woke, shivering in the strange bed, the strange room, terrified as a child until a wet tongue licking her face brought her back to reality.

It was early, she found, glancing at the luminous clock, but she knew she would not sleep again. A longing to be outdoors seized her, and dressing hurriedly, she took Dragon into the park. The artificial sunlight had not yet been switched on, and the autumn morning was smudged with mist, a mist reflected in her mind. She had known many worse nightmares, and yet the effect of this one was the most curious unease. She did not want to investigate it; she wanted to put it completely out of her mind.

"Good morning," said a voice from the mist. She turned, half relieved and half resentful at the intrusion, and saw the middle-aged man named Richard walking up behind her. "It's not often I find other guests about at this hour; I hope it's not sleeplessness that has brought you."

"Partly," said Clare, falling into step beside him. "And partly Dragon."

"Of course, the little dog. He'll go with you, I suppose?"

She did not understand for a moment, then said shortly:

"Yes. He'd pine himself sick without me."

"I have three more days," said Richard. "I feel rather like I used to feel at school, counting up the time until the holidays."

She glanced at him, struck once again by the fantastic situation, and by the expression he had used – "the holidays." A queer term, surely, for annihilation. She said lamely:

"I don't seem to be able to get used to the idea – I mean, the martyr angle. It's all so new – "

"New? Why, most of the great pagans glorified what we call self-elimination. Ancient history has been a hobby of mine, and it amuses me to hear my contemporaries hailing as new so many things with which our pagan ancestors were quite familiar. Take legalized abortion, for instance. Remember what Aristotle said about that? – 'When we decide between leaving children to die or bringing them up, this is the principle to follow: No deformed child is ever to be reared. If a man finds that he is going to have twice as many children as he can cope with, yet the local laws and customs forbid the abandoning of children, he is to anticipate the difficulty and procure abortion'."

She made no comment, and he continued kindly:

"This is the worst hour of the day, you know, before our early tea. Everything gets into its proper proportion after that. Of course one can always ring and ask for something, but I don't; I am plagued by the ridiculous idea that at this hour, by myself out-of-doors, I may suddenly come upon the answer. Of course I never do, but on the other hand I can't rid myself of the haunting suspicion that there *is* an answer. Ah well, three more days and I shall know, one way or the other."

"You don't mean you think that – well, you'll go on?"

"I don't know really. It's just that I would like there to be some sort of pattern in the story; 'winding up the estate' is the phrase which keeps recurring to me; foolish, isn't it? I'm a scientist, cursed with a mind which for ever seeks to know the reason why."

"But then you, of all people, surely must have found the pattern. I thought Science explained everything – "

"The commonest error of the unscientific," he interrupted, yet without rudeness. "Well, it doesn't signify."

They walked on in silence for a while, Clare occasionally whistling to Dragon who, in a strange place, was apt to explore too far, lose himself and get into a panic. Presently she asked:

"What sort of answer are you looking for?"

"I want to know why, the more we conquer Nature, the more we discover for our comfort and security, so much the more unhappy we seem to become."

Then, suddenly raising his hat, he turned and strode away into the mist.

(ii)

"Everything gets into its proper proportion after early morning tea," he had said. But it was not quite like that with Clare.

By the time she had drunk her tea, and had eaten the breakfast brought up to her room, she was conscious of a return of that queer lightness of body and relaxation of mind which she had experienced the previous evening. As she made up her face before the mirror, she saw that she had a half-smile on her lips, giving her a resemblance to the other "guests."

For an instant she knew a prick of uneasiness; then she brushed it aside. She had enough troubles without imagining more, and Richard had been right when he dismissed all worries with, "It doesn't signify." People who came to Fremley Manor were in sight of the end of all cares; was that not why they were here? Anyway it was a glorious autumn morning, which was something to be thankful for, and she would spend it exploring the park with Dragon.

The park blazed with tawny bracken, through which wound little paths. Dragon, who loved strange places, was in his element, disappearing into the miniature forest, busily wriggling his body, so like the bracken in colour, between the stout stems, his tail a periscope. His aliveness hurt her terribly, his trust which she soon must betray. But that was sentimental and irrational; for so long now there had been just the two of them, and the cruelty would have been to leave him behind. There would be no pain whatsoever, and no fear, for he would die in her arms.

And suddenly, as she thought of that, she began to cry.

Except for the breakdown immediately after her arrival here yesterday, she had not wept for months; it had been a relief denied her. She leant against a gate now, and laying her arms along it, put her head down on them and let the tears have their way. Dragon, heedless of this human misery, capered among the bracken, his strong thin tail waving stiffly, his nose earthy from digging. She was so abandoned in venting her grief, which was like a spiritual vomiting, that the man who had come up behind her had to speak twice before she was aware of his presence.

She raised a wet face and stared resentfully at Stephen, hands in pockets, pipe in mouth, his rather saturnine face expressionless.

"Better to stay in the house for the first day or two," he remarked, taking his pipe from between his teeth and studying it. "Lonely walks and all that sort of thing – they're bad. Come on, I'll stroll back with you, and we'll play darts or something."

"Would you mind?" snapped Clare, blowing her nose and hating him, "It happens that I want a lonely walk this morning." He did not move, and a sudden intolerable suspicion stabbed her. "Were you following me on purpose? Are we all under some sort of surveillance here?"

He placed a hand lightly under her arm and walked her on, whistling to the dog. As he remained silent, she added insistently:

"Are you a – a guest?"

"No," said Stephen. "Sort of private eye and general shepherd of martyrs. Have to see that the little dears are comfortable and occupied, and not brooding, y'know. They don't, of course, after a day or two, but some of 'em, just at first, are a bit tricky. Did you drink your tea this morning?"

"Yes. What has that got to do with it?"

"I'll give you a cocktail when we get in. It's always opening-time at Cowards' Hall."

She wrenched her arm from his and faced him.

"I suppose a job of that sort does attract the sadists; and what a paradise it must be for people of your type! Looking after human derelicts – "

"Tut tut! That's rank heresy, y'know. Don't you let the Lord High Executioner catch you saying things like that."

She shrank back, trembling with mingled fury and nausea; the relief of tears had vanished, and so had that pleasant relaxation of mind.

"It would be best if you didn't let him hear you call him that – if, as I suppose, you're referring to Mr Reddington, or to talk about 'Cowards' Hall', if you want to keep your job."

"I'm Mr Reddington's blue-eyed boy," said Stephen, pausing to relight his pipe. "And so popular with our dear martyrs. Didn't you notice that last night?"

"I can't imagine why. Call the people who come here what you like, the fact remains that they have reached the limit of misery and are entitled to some kind of consideration. Haven't they gone through enough without having you sneer at them, fed your sadism on them – "

"I don't think I'm sadistic, y'know," interrupted Stephen, in a tone which made him seem to be pondering on the likelihood. "Disillusioned – entirely; disappointed – yes; sadistic, no, I honestly don't think so. But you're intelligent enough, my dear girl, surely, to realize that half our guests don't come here because they have 'reached the limit of misery'."

"Perhaps you can suggest another reason?"

"Plenty. I'm in a position to know, you see, having studied the victims of our human abbatoir for six months now. Make it not only legal to commit suicide (excuse the dirty word), but praiseworthy, and you could expect a rush to shuffle off this mortal coil. Human nature remains human nature even in the age of Universal Brotherhood, and human nature, my good wench, loves to get itself into the papers, to see its name in lights, to succeed in winning notoriety at any price. You had it in the old days when the police were deluged with false confessions of some juicy murder."

"I've never thought it witty to be cynical."

"And apart from self-importance, there's boredom," went on Stephen, disregarding this remark; "you wouldn't believe to what lengths that can drive a person. Before self-elimination came along, boredom had to be staved off with new vices, each of which palled like the last; but there aren't any vices now, no forbidden fruit. And then of course they've taken away competition, and the novelty of travel and exploration; there's nothing left to explore since space-travel proved that the planets were uninhabitable, and competition has become just another dirty word. And lastly there's the sheer downright gutlessness which has become the norm. The world isn't just what you want it to be, so get out of it, if the psychos have given you up."

"And what do you suggest instead?"

"Not to give *yourself* up, I suppose."

They walked on in silence, Stephen placidly smoking, Clare cold in mind and body. At last she said:

"I can't think why you talk to me like this. I might report you to Mr Reddington."

"You're not that gutless."

"I'm not gutless at all!" she snapped, stung by the repetition of the word. "It's all very well for you to be smug, but I tell you it isn't easy to do what I'm doing – "

"It's much more bloody difficult to do what you're *not* doing – live."

"And what's the sense of living, will you tell me that?" She was facing him again, her fists clenched to prevent them from trembling, her eyes frantic. "Don't you think I've tried? I'm not bored, and I don't want the loathsome sore of notoriety of which you spoke. I'm just a failure – "

"The great Clare Bentley, S A, a failure? Surely not."

"My work means nothing; nothing means anything; except – "

"Luv!" he groaned. "I might have known it. Another love-lorn lady. Oh Hebrides! Such an *unusual* story – all passion, nothing like it since Antony and Cleopatra."

She stared at him for a moment, her eyes dark with hate. Then she turned abruptly and began to walk in the opposite direction, Dragon, who had sensed that something was amiss, barking round her. Inexorably the man followed.

"Look, Clare, don't be a fool. You've made your bed, your last bed, and you've got to lie on it. You're not so gutless as to run away, y'know, and even if you were, you couldn't. No ration books, no identity card, officially written off the list of citizens, already on the list of the new martyrs – no, you can't run away. So come back and have that cocktail. Sorry I was a bloody boor, but you've disappointed me, you really have, and I thought I was the complete cynic by this time."

"What do you mean – disappointed you?"

"Aha! That pricked your vanity, didn't it? As a matter of fact, I've always admired you as an artist. You have, or rather you had, integrity, rare in these days. And last night I liked the look of you; proud, kind, with the virtue of compassion – rare again. But you've pity for yourself, bags of it, and we've enough self-pity here as it is."

"Then would you kindly have a little compassion on your side, and leave me alone? I don't want a drink, and I don't want your company."

"Afraid you'll have to have the drink. The Lord High Ex. will see to that if I don't; he has an uncanny knack of discovering guests in distress."

She stopped again, a belated suspicion reawaking.

"Is there something special about the drinks here?"

He did not answer, his eyes downcast as he held another match to his pipe.

"So there is! I thought there must be. And the tea, too – everything. What is it?"

"You wouldn't know its name, but it's a very harmless, very kindly dope, a mercy-drug. Ever had an operation? Well, then, you may remember that before going down to the theatre they gave you a shot, just to make you calm. Same thing, or as near as makes no matter, that you have in your tea and cocktails here, adjusted to the individual patient. Pretty considerate, when you come to think of it. When we're merciful today, we don't do things by halves. A fortnight in perfect comfort for self-eliminators wouldn't be perfect comfort for those who have nerves or imagination, or who are infirm of purpose. So we make sure that their nerves are quieted and their imagination dulled, and that they're in a state in which they just can't be infirm of purpose. It's one of my jobs to gauge the amount each guest needs, and I flatter myself I've become pretty expert. But you're a hard case; I'll have to double the dose with you."

"You'll stop it altogether."

He put his hand on her arm again, forcing her to pause; but this time both touch and tone were gentler as he said:

"Look, Clare, I paid you the compliment of telling you the truth about this. The guests are not supposed to know, because it might upset their vanity. But you haven't that sort of vanity."

"Thank you for nothing. I have, however, some sort of pride. What I came here to do, I will do in my full senses. If you don't stop putting this stuff into my drinks, I shall report to Mr Reddington the conversation we've had this morning."

His face hardened.

"A spot of blackmail, eh?"

"Call it whatever you like."

"You'd never have the guts to go through with it, girl, unless you had your dope."

"Just now you implied that it was gutless to go through with it at all."

"Fair enough. But why torture yourself unnecessarily? Self-preservation's a strong instinct, Clare; you'll find that out as the day draws nearer. Come now, be sensible – "

"I've said my last word on the subject. And don't think I shan't know if you persist in doping me. I'm on my guard now."

"The Lord High Ex. will know if I'm *not* doping you. He's got an eye like a hawk."

"Don't worry. I can act."

He stared at her for a moment; then he said, slowly and bitingly:

"All right, love-sick heroine. You shall die without the bandage round your eyes in the best romantic manner. But don't blame me if the next fortnight is a very special sort of Hebrides."

(iii)

She did know at once, without being able to give a reason for it, since there was no difference in the taste, that Stephen was keeping his side of the bargain; the China tea brought up to her room that afternoon was China tea and nothing more. And the same applied to the gin and tonic she drank in the Bar of Happiness later.

For the first time since Michael left her she was conscious of a faint exhilaration; she had issued a challenge, and it had been accepted. She was not a silly lamb taking itself to the slaughter; she was an intelligent human being deliberately eliminating herself in the full possession of her senses, and she would prove to the odious Stephen that it was not vanity, or boredom, or gutlessness that had brought her to Fremley Manor.

But she must keep her side of the bargain too; she sat easy and relaxed in her chair at one of the little tables, answered Mr Reddington's greeting with a placid smile and a dreamy politeness, and prepared to enter into conversation with her two companions, the extremely handsome lady named Margaret, and Enid, so like a miniature poodle.

For a while it was Enid who held the field. In the pre-Brotherhood days she would have been, Clare was sure, a fervent vegetarian, nuclear disarmer, spiritualist, or devotee of Nature Cure. She quoted from little books she had read about the glories of self-elimination; she had been an early member of the Euthanasia Association; she had all the zeal of the missionary, and she was completely without a sense of humour.

"The cleanliness of it, the decency, that's what attracts me so much," babbled Enid, taking little bird-like pecks at her orange-squash. "You're not old enough, dear," she went on, addressing Clare, "to remember funerals – "

"Meaning that I am," interjected Margaret, dryly, but obviously huffed.

"No, no, of course not," cried Enid, embarrassed. "I mean of course neither of you would remember real funerals, and that's what I'm talking about. Cremation was bad enough, I know – those dreadful buildings with huge smoking chimneys like an old-fashioned factory, and the distress of the relatives when the coffin – ugh! what a hateful word! – was slid through the doors into the furnace. But think what it was like when they actually buried people in the ground! Bodies, dear, decomposing bodies lying about all over the place, and people living next-door to cemeteries, and the dreadful thought of your loved ones being eaten by worms, not to speak of the diseases. And it went on right up to the Last World War, though by that time the majority of people were being cremated. Even then there had to be coffins, and if you wanted the ashes (fancy anybody actually wanting ashes!) you had to wait till they had cooled, and then for all you knew you might get someone else's. Can you imagine any sane person living with a dead body's ashes on their mantelpiece?"

"But aren't there any ashes now?" asked Clare, feeling a kind of macabre interest.

"There's nothing left, dear, *nothing at all*," hissed Enid, learning forward and positively gloating with cleanly fervour. "Even the dust disappears in eight and a half minutes. I'll lend you dear Mrs Amy Forbes' book on it, if you're interested; to me it's one of the great wonders of

Science, and what a complete answer to the Christian nonsense about dust to dust and ashes to ashes! You see, they found in the early days, when they used to sprinkle the ashes on the earth, the early nuclear days I mean, that it did something bad to the soil, so that was one of the reasons why it was such a triumph when they found they could disintegrate us without leaving even dust. But oh the cleanliness of it! That's the most glorious thing to me."

"But you can't mean," floundered Clare, completely bewildered, "that you decided to eliminate yourself only because – well, I'm afraid I haven't a clue what you mean, and it seems discourteous to ask."

"Oh no, dear, no!" Enid assured her, leaning even closer, and breathing orange-squash-and-mercy-drug into Clare's face. "I *like* to tell people why. I never could bear any sort of dirt, dear; even as a child I was for ever washing my hands. Years hence, Man will have conquered dirt, just as he's conquering everything else that's nasty, but meanwhile there are still dreadful things like *lavatories*. I got to the point when I couldn't bear it any longer, and oh, it's such a comfort to me to know that when I'm gone not the teeniest bit of me will remain to offend others. *You* must feel that, dear," she added to Margaret, with an ingratiating smile. "You would hate anything *ugly* to be left when you go, now wouldn't you?"

"I shouldn't know, so I couldn't care less," drawled Margaret.

"But other people would see – "

"*I* shouldn't." She turned her rather insolent eyes on Clare. "You puzzle me, you know. How old are you – thirty-eight?"

"Thirty-two," replied Clare shortly, at the same time conscious of how ridiculous it was that in such a place and in such circumstances she should mind being taken for older than she was.

"H'm, you could be," pursued Margaret, lazily scrutinizing her. "You look older because your face is so drawn. Well, with plastic surgery and drugs you've at least ten years of real beauty ahead of you; you'd qualify for the special treatments, you know, for you've excellent bone structure and really lovely eyes. Why didn't you apply?"

"I don't understand."

"To the Ministry of Beauty, of course," snapped Margaret, obviously irritated. "You'd have passed all the tests, I'm pretty sure, and could have had all the very latest injections and so on. It infuriates me when I see women of your age and looks giving up."

"You don't mean that beauty can be something to live for? I mean, one's own personal beauty?"

"What else? Look at me; how old would you say I am?"

A tricky question always, even here, and especially, it seemed, with this woman. Clare studied her, and answered at last with honesty:

"Perhaps my age."

For the first time Margaret smiled, and it was not the unnatural smile common to the inmates of Fremley.

"Fifty-five, my dear, nearly fifty-six. Oh, they could have kept me going for another ten years, I suppose; look at some of our actresses. But I lost the urge for it; I just couldn't face the necessary stepping-up of the treatments. Besides, though I suppose I oughtn't to say this," she went on, lowering her voice, "after a certain age all the treatments give only a veneer. I know, because I've made a life-long study of my looks, and I can see, or I think I can see, which amounts to the same thing, a kind of falsity. It comes after the change, I believe; still, they're working hard on that, especially this Japanese, what's-his-name, and in time there won't be any menopause. Too late for me, but I can't grumble. I've had the most intense pleasure from a lifetime of being beautiful, and what more can any woman ask? Which brings me back to what I was going to ask you originally; why on earth do you want to eliminate?"

"I'm sorry," said Clare, rising abruptly, "but I'll have to take Dragon out. He's fidgeting."

(iv)

Bravado, she thought, sheer, silly bravado, to refuse this drug. Damn it all, I'd had enough suffering without going out of my way to ask for more; it's just perverse to make these two weeks a torment when they might have been pleasant, when I might have found a measure of peace.

But she was proud and obstinate, and catching Stephen's sardonic glance upon her several times that evening, her obstinacy grew. The great thing, she told herself, is that the end is in sight; already a day and a night have passed; and then she remembered Richard, counting the time like a schoolboy crossing off dates before the holidays. Only there aren't any holidays to look forward to; nonsense, she rebuked herself sharply; there was the best and only holiday for such as she, oblivion.

"Quite sure you are going to sleep, dear?" inquired Mrs Reddington, rustling into Clare's bedroom in a taffeta evening-gown, turning back the covers to see that the blanket was at the right temperature, plumping up the pillows. "You look a little tired this evening. I think perhaps you should have some hot milk."

Clare stopped herself as she was about to refuse. For one thing it might arouse suspicion that she was avoiding the drug, and for another – well, the night was long, and who knew or cared whether her resolution would prove sufficient to face it? When Mrs Reddington had rustled out and in again with a beaker of hot milk, and had finally said good night, Clare bathed, put on a robe, and deliberately ignoring the drugged milk, sat down on the cushioned window seat, drawing back a curtain and looking out into the moonlit night.

"It's much more bloody difficult to do what you're *not* doing – live."

That was what Stephen had said, touching a lingering doubt in her own mind, something the psychiatrists had assured her was a guilt-complex. Fundamentally honest, she could not rid herself of this suspicion that at least part of the wreck of the Michael-Clare relationship was her own fault. Michael had been honest with her from the start; he was prepared to give her, and had given her, all he had to give. There were long periods when she had accepted this limitation, and then they were at one; then came the lover-friend relationship, so infinitely precious.

But then, she thought, just when I was sure I had conquered them, those awful black moods would pounce on me, a hunger he could not satisfy, a hunger turning to resentment. He could no more understand it than I could understand this thing he had about his wife.

Shipwrecked we were continually, either upon that hateful rock, or in the fog of my resentment; never could we reach the harbour where we would be. If I could have rationalized my own yearning, when like a child I cried for the moon, there would have been a harbour, though not the one I longed for when I set out to sea. Friendship would have grown between us, so that when ultimately Barbara came home, though I had to sacrifice the lover I could have retained the friend. Unsatisfactory, yes, but better, oh far better, than nothing. I knew that, deep inside me; yet I could not master my absurd longing for the entire dominion of his heart.

It doesn't matter, of course, she thought drearily. It's all over. But if I could even yet understand the nature of that yearning which sexual passion could not satisfy, it would tie up the raged ends, wind up the estate, as Richard phrased it, complete the picture, and I could go out in peace.

She was still sitting at the window, looking out into the milky moonlight, not seeing it, facing only the blank wall of her problem, going round and round like a squirrel in its cage. But then she did see something with her bodily eyes, and it was like a mocking answer. Silent and streamlined, a dove-grey van moved down the drive, and the moonlight showed her the white slogan painted on it, the motto of the Euthanasia Laboratories:

Peace Unlimited.

With one dry sob she flung back the curtain, hurried across to the table, emptied the drugged milk down her throat, and slumped into bed. Beneath the eiderdown a thin strong tail began to thump.

It must have been an extra strong dose of the drug, for when she woke at last she was aware immediately that she had overslept. Dragon, always a late riser, was fidgeting about the room, shaking himself with that odd rattling sound he made, as though he wore mail.

She felt a little sick, and strangely beaten in spirit; she was putting out her hand for her watch, when there was a soft tap on the door, and Mrs Reddington entered, bearing a tray. Mrs Reddington did not rustle as she had last night; she was dressed in an immaculately pleated skirt and a twin-set of softest wool. She was so exactly her husband's complement, a lady from an old advertisement, the model for some expensive store's fashions for the not-so-young, or the result of a tonic for the over-forties.

"I told them not to wake you, dearest," tenderly murmured Mrs Reddington. "I peeped in myself earlier, and you were sleeping oh so peacefully; I was sure last night you were over-tired. Now I have brought you some tea, and you just stay there till you feel inclined to get up. I will take this sweet little rascal out to spend his pennies and pay his call (will you come with auntie, poppet?), and bring him back to you. I shan't draw your curtains yet awhile, for I am quite certain that you will sleep for another few hours."

And you are quite wrong, thought Clare, listening to Dragon's strangely heavy footsteps going down the corridor. She was no longer in the least sleepy, but that synthetic calm and clarity had returned to her mind; she was like someone who goes to sleep with a problem, and wakes to find it solved.

No, not solved. Only presented under a new aspect. Stephen had sneered at the reason that had brought her to Fremley; such an *unusual* story, he had said, meaning, how commonplace! Well, perhaps it was. The story of a tormented, frustrated, angry love, a series of exhausting quarrels and reconciliations; and not just because of Barbara. What she, Clare, had yearned for was of the same nature as that for which Richard yearned, and Felicity, and poor Mrs Smith. They called it by different names, but at least it was something that an earthly utopia was unable to give. It was the satisfaction of what used to be called the soul...

Clare moved restlessly on her pillows, the pleasant calm receding. For suddenly she realized that her thoughts were taking a preposterous turn. Once admit that there was a thing called the soul, and certain conclusions inevitably followed. Man was not, after all, autonomous, and the Christians just possibly might be right.

She got out of bed and began dressing, just for the sake of something to do. For out of nowhere, as it seemed, the memory of her strange dream had returned to her, the dream of being pursued by Something which wore the face of Linda and yet was not Linda; Something inexorable and effortless, for which there was neither time nor space.

Chapter Six

(i)

November 1st was the new Remembrance Day, and was celebrated throughout the country with special rites. The names of the martyrs of self-elimination of the past twelve months were read out in the various districts where they had lived; there were lectures, hymns, processions, and wreaths were laid on the Martyrs' Memorials. The Prime Minister addressed the nation on television, and the faint Birmingham accent of APS was followed by the Glasgow voice of the Minister of Uplift.

At Fremley Manor, as at the other Homes of Rest, the day was observed with particular solemnity, and in the Television Room in the evening, Mr Reddington treated his guests to one of those homely but inspiring talks for which he was so much admired. He read a passage from the Brotherhood Bible, so admirably adapted from the Christian Scriptures. What used to be called the Old Testament had been jettisoned entirely, being regarded as a mere piece of ancient history (though it was still occasionally quoted to prove the horribleness of the Christian God), and the New Testament had been skilfully cut and altered to bring it into line with Humanitarianism.

" 'I and my Father are one,' the Carpenter of Nazareth is reported to have said," intoned Mr Reddington, "and his

94

poor deluded peasant followers took this to mean that he was the son of a supernatural father, instead of what he obviously meant, that Man was God. Our modern Christians, that handful of poor cranks in the reservations, tell us that we cannot pick out the bits that we agree with in his teaching, and reject the rest. But, my dear friends, if Man is God, he can accept or reject whatsoever his reason bids him. He is not ashamed to incorporate into his philosophy the truths of one which was largely mistaken... "

In the midst of this sermon, which she found perversely embarrassing, Clare became aware of a slight commotion in the row of chairs behind her. Glancing back, she saw that a new "guest," a man who had arrived, apparently, only just before the lecture, since she had not seen him at dinner, had risen and was making his way, hurriedly and clumsily, past his neighbours' knees. His demeanour suggested that he was ill, and she was relieved to se the tall figure of Stephen rise from his place near the door, and hurry after the stranger.

Mr Reddington himself took no notice, but continued tranquilly, and it must be admitted, unctuously, on the glorious Army of Martyrs as foretold in the Book of Revelation. Some of these noble men and women, he was proud to know, were gathered here this evening, for whom sorrow and mourning should soon be no more. His audience, relaxed and submissive after their day's ration of mercy-drug, basked in his praise.

Clare did not drink her bedtime milk that night, but evidently there must have been some of the drug in her cocktail in her Bar of Happiness, for she slept as soon as she got into bed. She woke to hear a clock strike one, and immediately was conscious of a stealthy footstep outside her door.

Her mind, defenceless at this hour, reacted with crude physical fear. Like a child waking in a dark night-nursery, she was the prey of reasonless terror. They're going to do it now, she thought, forgetting that "it" was something she had come here to do herself. They've decided that I'm not fit to have the usual fortnight. I ought to have realized that I don't look properly doped. "The Lord High Executioner." Stephen's nickname for Mr Reddington suddenly assumed a sinister guise; he was there, outside her door, in a white coat, masked like a surgeon, with a little hypodermic syringe in his hand...

Her own hand slipped inside the eiderdown, and found Dragon's smooth, plump flank. Oh not like this, she begged silently, not in the small hours of the morning, secretly, forcibly, before my time. Of a sudden material things became infinitely precious, the warmth of bed, the light of the sun (even if it were only an artificial sun), the things she had believed to hold no further comfort. Her mind scurried round, a trapped animal, yet her own mind still, the torturer from which she had desired escape, but not before she was ready. It's against the law, she thought wildly; then cried out something as the door softly opened, and a man's figure was outlined in the light from the corridor.

"Ssh! it's only me," said Stephen's voice. "Who the Hebrides did you think it was? We don't have burglars at Cowards' Hall." He came and sat down on the side of the bed. "Feel like a spot of libido?"

She began to laugh hysterically, too much the product of her age to be insulted, furious with herself for her recent panic and even more furious with him as the cause of it. With relief she discovered another and less humiliating reason for being angry with him.

"You put some of the dope into my cocktail last evening. It's no use denying it. You've broken your pact with me,

96

and you've only yourself to blame if I break my side of it. In any case I feel I ought to tell Mr Reddington about the sort of things you've been saying to me; you're no fit person for the job, and it's intolerable that you should inflict further suffering on the people who come here. It's all very well to – "

"Oh belt up!" Stephen interrupted rudely. "Just like a woman – yap, yap, yap! And do what you like about blabbing to the Lord High; I'm fed up with the job anyway. But for Brotherhood's sake don't kid yourself that you're concerned about other people. There's only one person you care two hoots about, and that's Clare Bentley."

He got off the bed, stalked to the table beside the fire, took a cigarette from the silver box, and flung himself into the armchair. Dragon, roused from slumber, leapt down and on to his knees; Clare had noticed before that the dog, ordinarily indifferent to everyone except herself, appeared to have conceived a special affection for Stephen. She lay still, jealously watching Dragon who, squirming with joy, was bestowing large wet kisses on the man's face, his hand-like forepaws, with their long black nails, planted on Stephen's chest.

"Well, go on, go on," said Stephen, fondling Dragon and addressing Clare. "The bell's beside your bed; ring for the Lord High Ex., denounce me, and get it over with. You can say I tried to rape you, too; that would pander to your love of finding some grievance, and it'd give the Lord High the Hebrides of a kick. His trusted henchman a wolf in sheep's clothing."

"Oh please stop," begged Clare wearily. She got out of bed, put on her robe, and came and sat down opposite him. "Why did you come here actually?"

"Partly because I was a bloody fool and was worried about you; and not, though you won't believe it, because I was afraid that your muling and puling would give the game away that you weren't having your ration of dope. Got to have some sort of dope here, Clare, you take it from me, and I thought the odd spot of sex might help. After all, I'm not all that unattractive, am I?"

She laughed again, but this time naturally. Her uninvited guest responded with a grin which made him look suddenly very attractive indeed. She asked, reaching out for a cigarette:

"And partly you came because – ?"

"I needed to talk to someone in their right mind. I've had a pretty bloody awful evening with the old geezer next-door to you, our new guest."

"Was that the man who went out of the Television Room during Mr Reddington's sermon?"

"Uha. There aren't many people who come here I'm sorry for; but I'm bloody sorry for him. He's all right now; he's had a huge dollop of the dope, but the Lord High Ex. and I had a game, I can tell you, before he passed out. I thought at one point he was going to bash the Lord High; that really would have been something."

"You don't like the Lord High, I gather."

"He's the kind of thing I'd like to put my foot on and squash – like that," said Stephen, suiting the action to the word. "But he's my boss, and my bread and butter, and there you are."

"Why did you take the job, Stephen?"

He did not answer for several moments, and she supposed he was meditating some biting reply. But when at last he spoke, it was in a pensive tone, and without looking at her.

"My hobby, if you like, has always been people – no, my good girl, I am *not* an amateur psychoanalyst. I don't want any of your systematically organized knowledge of human nature; I'm not interested in cases, just in men and women. Sounds corny, doesn't it?"

"I don't think so."

"The human race has always seemed to me the most interesting thing on this earth (though by no means the most attractive), and I wanted to discover what people are like when all the barriers are down, when all the modern methods of treating the mind have failed. Well, by and large, I found we're a pretty poor lot, and after a week or two here I thought I'd become the complete cynic. Then I came across a few 'guests' who made me think again, people who really might have been something worthwhile if our brave new world hadn't proved too strong for them, people with character and what used to be called ideals. And so I'm more puzzled than ever, and no nearer finding the answer."

"The answer," she repeated slowly. "That's what the man named Richard said he was looking for. He wanted to know why we're no nearer happiness, further from it, he said, with all our modern inventions and our freedom from war and want and pain. But surely people *are* happy – except, of course, those who come here."

"Are they indeed? Ever look around you at the faces you saw before you came to Fremley? No, I don't suppose you did, my complete egotist."

She swallowed that, because she was interested.

"It's only because old attitudes of mind take time to die out completely," she argued, lighting a fresh cigarette from the stump of the old one. "People aren't adjusted yet. A generation or two hence won't be plagued by wanting to find the answers to questions which don't really exist, like whether there's after we die, and so on."

"You're very glib. I think you must have been mugging up some of the Lord High Ex.'s little tracts."

"I have not!" snapped Clare. "I'm merely stating the obvious."

"And the obvious is inevitably true?" he asked dryly. Then he went on, leaning forward and looking at her intently: "But how do you know there's nothing after death? All your scientists can't *prove* it. Mind you, I'm not saying that there is; I think it's extremely unlikely. But I don't *know* that when the atomic pencil has touched that carcass sitting there in that chair and calling itself Clare Bentley, and has turned it into a handful of dust which again will disintegrate and disappear in eight and a half minutes, the Clare Bentley who thinks and feels and loves and suffers isn't somewhere else."

"So what?" she asked with false contempt.

"My dear girl, don't pretend to be sillier than you are. So this: If – I say *if* – by any possible or impossible chance, the real Clare Bentley does go on after her carcass has disappeared, the self-elimination is pointless. You're not escaping as you thought you were. Moreover, there *is* something more important than material comfort and the conquest of disease and even of war, something that used to be called the spirit. And about the spirit we know nothing, where it goes, what it wants, what part it plays in human existence. In fact, we may be leaving out of our calculations the biggest thing of all. Now you say that in a generation or two we won't be plagued by wanting to find the answers to such problems. You might just as well say that in a generation or two we shall be like cows, incapable of any emotions. But I can't help wondering whether any material utopia will ever completely satisfy any human creature."

"You don't think a spiritual one would, surely?"

"I haven't a clue."

She moved restlessly. She was disquieted by the fact that he was voicing some of her own thoughts in bed only yesterday.

"Well, did it?"

"There never was such a thing. As I understand it, the Christians looked beyond this world for their satisfaction. They had not here an abiding city, as they said."

"Yes, Stephen, but material security and freedom from war and want are undeniable blessings; and far from concentrating on them, the Christians taught that they were relatively unimportant."

"Well, they can't be all that important, or you and the rest of our honoured guests wouldn't be here. And don't tell me you're only a small minority. Statistics prove that our new martyrs are alarmingly on the increase."

"But heaps of people committed suicide, as they called it, in the old days, Stephen," she argued, feeling that it was desperately vital to convince him, though she couldn't tell why, oblivious of the strangeness of this conversation with a man she did not like in her bedroom in the small hours of the morning, "and many more would have done so only that they were afraid, or else because it was regarded as dishonourable and a stigma on their families."

"So we solved that problem by making it a virtue and a noble act and all the rest of the guff. Well, there it is. A queer lot, the human race; doesn't seem to know what it wants." He rose. "I must go and let you get some sleep."

"No, don't." Unconsciously she slipped down on to the hearthrug, in front of the fire, as she had sat so many times with Michael. "Stephen, do you know what you're saying? You despise me, and probably I deserve it; I despise myself at times. But don't be too harsh. I've only one crumb of comfort left; that when I go out I shall go out completely, that it will be the end of the suffering me."

"But you doubt it."

"I don't!" She swayed her body to and fro in a sort of agony. "Of course I don't. But I'm the product of the pre-Brotherhood age, and there are bits of my upbringing I can't entirely eradicate, and that makes it so hard. And there isn't any alternative to what I'm doing. My work's gone, you see; I'm not imagining that. There was no longer any life in it, any urge for creation. I'm useless, not only to myself but to others, to the world at large. Here was the only place left for me to go – "

"Except, of course, the Hebrides."

She stared at him, wondering whether he was mocking her, but except for a faintly quizzical look, his expression gave nothing away.

"I went there once," remarked Stephen, drawing out his pipe. "Mind this? It's the most extraordinary place."

"You *went* there?"

"By accident, of course. The plane I was in made a forced landing on one of the islands, and we were marooned there for twenty-four hours."

"How ghastly!"

"N-no, I wouldn't say that. Bizarre, but damned interesting."

"Like visiting an island of savages in the old days."

"Perhaps. Savages used to be happy, they say, and that's one of the things that most impressed me in the Hebrides. At least, I'd prefer the word 'joy'. That's a thing we've almost forgotten. Anyway, their happiness wasn't like anything I'd understood by that term. Oh, there was disease, and pain, and bloody hard work, and poverty, and all the rest of the ills we've done away with, but they had something, something very odd, for which I envied them. It was as if – how shall I put it? – they'd accepted life as it was, without forever wanting to alter it, and conquer Nature, and so on. They seemed to have got into a kind of rhythm; they had none of our feverishness."

He got up abruptly, putting the now sleeping Dragon into her arms.

"Really must go now, Clare. Look, do what you like about reporting me to the Lord High, but I'll have to give

102

you a spot of the dope. Sorry to wound your precious vanity, but you're not tough enough to carry through without it."

"No," she said, suddenly humble, "I'm not. But please let it be only enough to deaden and not kill thought altogether. I want to find the answer too, though I don't suppose I shall."

He smiled down at her; and for the first time there was genuine compassion in his face.

"Right. And by the way, be kind to our new guest, the wretched Peter, who's sleeping next door to you. He's one of the few 'martyrs' for whom I'm really sorry, and I don't think all the dope in the world is going to be enough for him without a spot of human kindness. He was a Catholic priest, and he's lost what he calls God. Good night."

(ii)

Clare was by nature a kind person, but it was not entirely this quality that made her linger about in the lounge-hall next morning in the hope of a talk with Peter. She had just realized the humiliating fact that in extreme wretchedness there is some comfort to be found in discovering a person in the like state. It was the only distraction she thought might turn her for a while from her hopeless quest in search of an answer to the unanswerable, and it would make the peculiar loneliness of despair a little less tormenting.

But no Peter had appeared by the time Dragon began pestering for his walk, so she was obliged to start out on a lonely ramble. Margaret, indeed, offered to go with her, when her revarnished nails were dry, but Clare found even her own company preferable to that of Margaret. She went out through a side door which gave directly on to the park: it was a grey, nondescript sort of morning, neither warm nor cold, and the artificial sunlight seemed more synthetic than ever.

Walking unseeingly through the bracken, which was black in places from recent frost, she began to play an absurd game she had invented which, dreary though it was, had kept her mind from complete derangement during those weary months when she was in the hands of the psychologists.

It consisted in repeating, over and over again, certain words, a sentence from a book, or a line from some poem, often trite and banal, not even correctly remembered, but precious for their single theme. "I am nearer my death today than ever I was before." "The hours fly fast, with each some sorrow flies, with each some shadow dies." "Fleet light, fleet breath, comes night, comes death." "This passes, all passes." It was a mechanical way of fixing her mind on the only longing she had left, and she used it when thought, going round and round in a circle, threatened to snap her self-control. She knew it was escapism, pure and simple, but permitted, and indeed recommended, by the psychiatrists.

She was hard at it now, walking along like a somnambulist, scarcely aware even of Dragon, when she came suddenly upon Peter, sitting on a fallen tree.

He sat hunched, both hands guiding his stick with which he appeared to be drawing a pattern in the soft earth in front of him. At first he did not look up, and Clare wondered whether it would be more tactful of her to walk past without appearing to notice him. But as she decided that it would be, he raised his head, slowly, his lips moved in a listless smile, and he made a motion to lift his hat before discovering that he wore none. Quite obviously he was heavily doped.

He was a slight man, below medium height, with untidy grey hair going thin on top, and a pair of extremely long eyebrows which made a thatch over his deep-set eyes, half concealing their expression. It had been a full face, but the flesh now hung in bags over the bones; the shaven jaw was blueish, telling of a strong beard. As Clare still hesitated whether or not to pause for conversation, her glance went instinctively to the pattern in the earth, and she saw that he had been drawing a cross, over and over again.

"I'm sorry," said Peter, like child caught out in some naughtiness.

She sat down beside him, strangely moved, though she could not have said why. He seemed a weak, pitiable sort of creature.

"One does all sorts of odd things here to pass the time," she said, throwing a stick to Dragon, who settled down to chew it. "I repeat words to myself to invoke an image; I was at it just now, a very childish trick, but it does work."

"A very old trick, and not childish in one sense, you know." He sat looking down, and unconsciously began drawing his crosses again. "A great deal of prayer was just that – repeating evocative words."

" 'Vain repetitions' – yes, I see."

"Filling the mind with associations and thus fixing it on God, that was what mattered. Even the great saints used it; St Francis of Assisi in particular."

Clare cleared her throat nervously. She was filled with curiosity, for this was the first Christian she had met, a very special sort of Christian, too, ex-member of the form of religion which had proved most antagonistic to Brotherhood, would not budge an inch from its dreadful dogmas, and reigned supreme in the reservations. And not only a Catholic, but actually a priest. She regarded him very much as her parents would have regarded a cannibal who had forsworn the eating of human flesh, but could not be entirely trusted.

"I don't really understand what you mean," she murmured. "I thought prayer was just asking for things. And surely you can't pretend that anyone answers?"

"If I ask you for something, and you say 'No', have I not been answered? Can't it be an answer unless it is 'Yes'?" he asked mildly.

This conversation is not going to get anywhere, she thought, and I ought to go. I'm muddled enough already. But instead, she picked up a twig, made to throw it to Dragon, then changed her mind and in her turn began to draw in the soft earth. He watched her for a while in silence, then observed:

"You are an artist."

"Well, yes, I was. Clare Bentley. I used to illustrate children's books."

"Do you remember the one you did on old myths? I have never forgotten your picture of St George."

She stared at him.

"Why is that? I don't think it was a particularly good picture."

"You believed in St George, you know. It was there in your drawing. I mean, the idea of his sainthood."

"Oh no! Not as the old idea of a saint, I mean. The book was meant to illustrate the theme that from remote ages Man has been groping after the world as it is now; the dragon was disease and war and all the rest, and St George was the new man, lord of the world – "

"That was not how you drew him. That was how you were meant to draw him. But you are an artist, and you reproduced only what you saw in your own mind."

"I saw nothing except a sort of superman," she said angrily, at the same time wondering why she should feel angry. Then, as he remained silent, she went on: "I'm sorry, I'm sort of upset this morning. I had a nightmare last night, and the curious thing is that it was exactly like one

I'd had my first night here, only this time I didn't see what it was that was chasing me. But everything else was the same; I had the absurd hope that if only I got into some fast moving mechanical thing, I could escape." She laughed apologetically. "There is nothing more boring than other people's dreams."

" 'To all swift things for swiftness did I sue'," he quoted softly, looking at her through the thatch of his great brows.

"What did you say?"

"It comes from *The Hound of Heaven* –

> *Clung to the whistling mane of every wind,*
> *But whether they swept, smoothly fleet,*
> *The long savannahs of the blue,*
> *Or whether, thunder-driven,*
> *They clanged His chariot 'thwart a heaven,*
> *Plashy with lightnings round the spurn o' their feet –*
> *Fear wist not to evade as Love wist to pursue.*

Perhaps the Hound will catch up with you at last."

Her mouth felt dry. She was oddly frightened. She had a vivid mental picture of Linda, Linda in her black dress, with an unlit cigarette between her pale lips, quoting that poem, babbling about being chased by something, about an uncomfortable Presence, *there* all the time, more real than tables and chairs. Controlling herself, Clare said:

"Please don't think me impertinent, but I've never understood how rational people could believe that there was some sort of Being up there" – she made a vague gesture towards the sky – "to whom one could talk, and who listened, and was interested and could help. Do *you* believe it?"

"I did once," he said, so low that she could scarcely catch the words.

"You mean it was just the way you were brought up," said Clare, feeling unreasonably disappointed. "Of course it must have been difficult for you to rid yourself of that sort of superstition if it was drummed into you all your youth. I suppose it's like when one begins to grow up and suddenly realizes that there aren't such things as fairies. I'm old enough to have believed in fairies, you see, and I can remember feeling sort of lost and horribly disillusioned when I learnt it was all nonsense."

"But you found something to put in their place?"

She glanced sharply at him. Had she only imagined that there was a hint of irony in the question?

"One doesn't need anything to put in the place of childish myths. One becomes mature, and finds – well, the real world."

"Which is not enough, it seems, Miss Bentley, to make you want to go on living in it, to keep you from despair."

She felt her whole body stiffen. This was heresy, pure and simple, but it was not this which had shocked her. Being addressed as "Miss Bentley" again seemed to whirl her back into the world to which she had said goodbye for ever; further than this she was too honest not to admit to herself that it was despair and not a lofty self-sacrifice which had brought her to Fremley Manor. She and many other "guests." How many really sought annihilation because they desired the happiness of their fellow men?

"You must forgive me for saying this," she said tartly, "but if reality has failed me, no less have your old-fashioned beliefs failed you."

"No," said Peter beginning to draw his crosses again. "I have failed them."

"I simply don't know what you mean by that."

He sighed, and shifted wearily on the log. Her kindness urged her to discontinue a conversation which obviously distressed him, but something more urgent than kindness compelled her to force it to a conclusion.

"You must forgive me," Peter said in his turn. "I believe they gave me some sort of drug last night, and there is a great fog in my mind. What I meant was, that my own acts, or rather perhaps my failure to make acts, has resulted in faith being withdrawn. I deliberately cut the telephone wires, if I may put it like that, between myself and my Creator; I am unable to communicate with Him, and I am too weak to try to mend those wires."

She almost laughed. Really, this was too absurd!

"But I always thought that God was supposed to be omnipotent. If He wants you to communicate with Him, He has only to pass a miracle and mend the wires."

He smiled without mirth.

"That opens up the whole doctrine of free will, and I'm afraid my mind is not clear enough to explain it to you. Besides, I don't believe in it myself now; I did when I was there – "

"There?"

His eyes slid a swift, strangely frightened glance at her from under the thatch of his brows, and she saw him lick his lips.

"I mean, I did believe it at one time," he said hurriedly. And then, obviously desperate to change the subject: "But I am sorry to have failed you, Miss Bentley; and more sorry to find you in a place like this."

"There is no hope anywhere!" she wailed suddenly, beating her hands together. "Neither from others nor in oneself can one find the answer. And so it must be that there is no answer, and it is only my egotism which makes me long to discover why and how I failed. What does it matter, after all, that one human being should fail herself, so long as she removes her unhappiness and failure from a world that is in the possession of the happy and the integrated?"

"You are repeating a lesson which you don't believe."

She said nothing. Peter sighed again, and went on with an effort:

"The scientists, they tell me, are seeking some method to control the emotions; one day, they hope, men and women will love only the objects officially lovable. I am glad I shall not be here to see that day if ever it comes. But I do not think it will come, Miss Bentley; I think that the human heart, fickle and weak and unreasonable though it is, will defeat those who have harnessed the forces of Nature and believe they have explored the mind."

He paused a moment, and looked at Dragon who, tired of his stick, was sitting beside his mistress, his exquisitely modelled head cocked a little on one side, his eyes adoring.

"Would you like it if that dog loved you only because he had been injected with some new drug which compelled him to do so, which left him no choice? And pray don't tell me," he added, before she could reply, "that the dog loves you now only because you feed him and are kind to him and take him for walks and so on, because you know you really are far too intelligent to use that sort of argument."

"I don't know why Dragon loves me," cried Clare, fighting tears, "and I don't know why I loved Michael, and I begin to feel that love is a curse because without it there would be no unhappiness."

"Yes," he said mildly, "it is unhappiness our poor old world is seeking to eradicate, and dimly that world realizes that to do so it must 'control' love, even as it has controlled everything else. But pain is the thorn of which love is the rose; if you prick your finger, will you abolish roses?"

She got up with a movement in which there was violence, and walked off without courtesy. Her feet erased the crosses he had been drawing in the earth.

Chapter Seven

(i)

It was raining when Clare took Dragon out for his walk that afternoon. Dragon hated the rain; he slouched along with his tartan mackintosh slewed to one side, walking as it were on tiptoe, often pausing to shake himself, and stepping delicately as a cat between the puddles. Clare for her part walked with her hands thrust into her pockets and her head bent. She did not even try to play her absurd word-game; she seemed to have got back into the numbed state in which she had arrived at Fremley Manor.

But presently she began to have the feeling that she was being followed, and followed in a furtive manner. She glanced nervously over her shoulder, and thought she caught a glimpse of a figure dodging among the trees. For a moment, so dazed and battered was her mind, she was seized with the ridiculous fancy that this was her dream come true; someone was pursuing her, and there was no escape. Then the prosaic and hateful explanation occurred to her; Stephen was shadowing her again. She whipped round suddenly, and called in a high shrill voice:

"I won't have it, I tell you! I won't have it!"

There then emerged from the trees, not Stephen, but the man called Peter. He slouched as dejectedly as Dragon, his grey hair ruffled by the wind, his hands clutched together as though in supplication. He stammered miserably:

"I – I've been trying to pluck up my courage to speak to you, Miss Bentley. I – I wasn't frank with you this morning."

He looked so desolate that she was seized with pity, though at the same time faintly nauseated. He fell into step beside her, and went on:

"When I said that I did believe in God once, when I was 'there', I wouldn't tell you where 'there' was. But I haven't sunk so low as that. I am still Peter, not Judas – not yet."

I believe he's mad, thought Clare, now really frightened. She had come a long way from the house, too far to call for help.

"I have denied, but not yet betrayed," he mumbled, speaking more to himself than to her, "though indeed the sin of Judas was not his betrayal but his despair of forgiveness."

"How can despair be a sin?" she asked, humouring him. "We don't do it willingly; we – "

"I have come from the Hebrides," he interrupted in a rush.

She stood stock still on the path, gaping at him. Either he was really mad, or else...

"But no one ever leaves the Hebrides; it's forbidden," she added feebly.

He gave her his mirthless smile.

"Did you really suppose that Christians would be content to stay in the reservations?"

"Well no, obviously nobody in their senses would be content to stay in places where there isn't anything to make life worth living."

"You misunderstand me. Our Lord Jesus Christ bade His followers go out and teach all nations, preach the Gospel to every creature. From that day to this, there have always been missionaries."

Before she could stop herself, she had given an hysterical laugh. He had said it quite seriously, but it was so utterly absurd. A handful of cranks daring to believe that they could convert this modern world! But then some of the implications of the idea occurred to her, and made her serious.

"But you know it's forbidden – it's high treason or something awful like that. I mean if you really are one of these missionaries. And how did you manage to get back to civilization – "

"How have men managed to penetrate into enemy territory throughout the ages?" he interrupted with a touch of impatience. "Every resistance movement from the beginning of time has had its ways and means, its passwords, secret sympathizers, codes and so on. But that's unimportant. I've lied and lied; but there is something about you that has compelled me to be honest – "

"Wait!" cried Clare, interrupting in her turn. "When did you come over?"

"Five months ago," he said, in a sombre tone she did not understand. "Yes," he added bitterly, "that's all it took to break me – five months."

She passed this over because she was suddenly obsessed by a personal longing.

"Then perhaps you knew my sister. She went to the Hebrides at the beginning of May. I don't know which island, of course, but I suppose in such a small community you must all know each other. Linda Coleworthy her name is. Oh do tell me – is she well? Is she terribly unhappy? Does she realize her awful mistake?"

He did not answer immediately. He had stopped in his walk and was regarding her with a strange sort of wistfulness.

"That's it," he muttered. "It was of her you reminded me this morning." And then aloud: "She is very well. She is very happy. She would not know what you meant by her 'mistake'. But you must be very anxious for her, Miss Bentley."

"How do you mean?"

"Surely you read the papers?"

"I – no, I haven't read them lately. You see – I was so obsessed with my own trouble that I'm afraid I – "

"Couldn't take much interest in other people's," he finished for her, but gently. "Infatuation, my dear child, commonly has two very unfortunate results. It robs us of our sense of humour, and it makes us egocentric."

"Yes, I know," said Clare. "But I do care about Linda, truly I do. Please tell me why you say I must be anxious about her."

"There has been a great deal of agitation in some quarters lately about the Christian reservations, as there was bound to be. For the world has always feared Christianity, even when it is reduced to a mere handful of men and women. There has been talk about 'plague-spots', about the danger of moral infection. They would like to despise us, to ignore us, but is seems they can't. And so – "

"And so?" she whispered; but already she knew.

"Oh, it will be done mercifully," he said, gently ironic. "In fact already they are speaking of the 'mercy bomb'. Our old friend euthanasia. The scientists in the Euthanasia Laboratories are working on a method of mass elimination, I believe. But why do I tell you this? Why torment you when you are – where you are?"

"But they can't do it! It's wicked!"

"Wicked? According to the new morality which, so I understood, you accept, it is strictly logical."

A tear splashed down on to her coat, and she put her fist against her trembling mouth.

"All right. I'm just a muddled thinker. I know. Oh why *did* you tell me? What can I do? I can't warn Linda. And you?" she shouted, turning on him. "What are you, coming over here to do what you call missionize, and ending up in a place like this? Doesn't that prove that Christianity's a lie?" she cried wildly.

"It proves only that I am weak and have failed. In just five months the pagan world has proved too strong for me, and I have denied my Lord."

He turned abruptly and walked away from her, shambling clumsily so that once or twice he stumbled over a tree root, splashing through the puddles, the embodiment of despair.

(ii)

"Ah, just the little lady I was looking for," said the gaily vigorous voice of Mr Reddington, as Clare crossed the hall to the stairs. "What would you say to having a quiet cup of tea and a cigarette in my sanctum? I have not had the privilege of a tête-à-tête since the evening of your arrival, Clare, and I am so anxious to hear how you are getting on. You'd like a wash, I'm sure, after your walk, and then you'll find me waiting for you in my room. And did he have a lovely ta-tas, did he?" inquired Mr Reddington, stooping to pat Dragon, who sniffed at his trouser ends, apparently disliked them, and began to ascend the stairs in a series of short leaps.

The invitation, Clare realized, was in fact a command, but she welcomed it. She knew perfectly well that the tea would be drugged, and she welcomed that too. After her encounter with Peter, company and dope were the only things to keep her sane. She did just wonder whether Mr Reddington had noticed that she was not as doped as she ought to be, had jumped to the right conclusion, and had given Stephen the sack. She was surprised to find that the possibility was faintly worrying, and not only because it might have been her fault.

Dragon ate little and often, and was extremely particular about his food. His tea, which consisted of a bowl of honeyed water, and a slice of dried brown bread and butter, was water, and a slice of dried brown bread and butter, was already set out on a tray in her room, the bowl bearing the word "DOG" in case there should be any mistake. Certainly the service at Fremley left nothing to be desired. Carefully removing the bread from the sheet of paper on which Clare had placed it, Dragon took it on to the carpet, grasped it firmly between his hand-like forepaws, and bit off the corners, spitting them out again before settling down, head on one side, to a steady chewing of the rest.

Combing her hair, Clare watched him with possessive fondness, this last friend. A piece of the hard bread lodged in one of his cheek pockets where he could not retrieve it, and it stuck out like a lump of toffee until she pushed it back into his mouth. The bread finished, he started on his drink, pausing every now and then to clear up the splashes with his tongue, for he was a very tidy animal.

Mr Reddington must have heard her step, for he had the door of his room open and was standing there to welcome her. He wore his doctor-priest air; he had all the time in the world, said his manner, to listen to tales of woe, to reassure the anxious patient, to advise the penitent troubled by scruples. Tea was set out in the bay window, through which streamed the artificial sunlight, and as he pulled out a chair for her, Mr Reddington quoted, inaccurately but reverently:

"'They have no longer any need of the sun, for the glory of God hath enlightened them', How little did the poor madman, John, imagine, that his 'vision' would come true two thousand years later! We have, indeed, no need of the sun, for Man has made his own light. Ah," he added, sipping his tea, "how good it is to relax."

"I expect you have had a busy day," murmured Clare, and immediately regretted the remark. For his busyness consisted in encouraging his "guests" to kill themselves.

"And you, my dear?" he asked gently. "I do hope that already you are finding some measure of peace?"

He went on talking, but she scarcely heard what he said. His mesmeric voice, the warm weight of Dragon in her arms, the cheerful crackle of the logs on the hearth, all combined to relax her. She wondered if the drug in her tea was some sort of a truth-drug, for presently she felt a strange urge to talk, to say things she had successfully resisted telling the psychiatrists. Mr Reddington was saying something about happiness, when she suddenly interrupted.

"I suppose there are people who never experience what I mean by happiness, and even for those who do it comes so rarely that afterwards you wonder whether you might not have imagined it. But you know you haven't, and when once you've experienced it, you can't be content with anything else. It is like discovering a country which you know is your true home, but to which you cannot come except by accident; it's like the old stories about people finding themselves in fairyland. I remember one occasion when I strayed into that blessed country, and I will describe to you what it was like... "

It was early March, a year after her first encounter with Michael in the train. He was coming to dinner and to stay the night, and she was walking on the Common in the morning, savouring the joy in store.

It seemed to her, even then, a day different from other days; some veil appeared to have fallen from her eyes, so that she saw the inner beauty of all familiar things. The

117

stripped look of the trees and of the ground, from which last year's leaves had been swept, had an air of completed preparation; it was like a stage-set already arranged for the play, and the birds, like shirt-sleeved musicians, were practising for the performance. There was as yet no hint of green, but the re trees had a new softness, with the shape of the buds very noticeable; branches were nigger-brown instead of black; some of the trunks looked like wet corduroy; and here and there the lamb's-tails, pale saffron caterpillars, hung from twigs. Little scatters of cloud were like fluff on the pale blue floor of the sky. One knew that very soon now the footlights and the limes would be turned on, and this pretty but colourless set would be transformed.

"Wonderful what an artist's eyes see," murmured a voice beside her.

She heard it only as though it were some meaningless remark of a passer-by, for, perhaps, as a result of the drug, she had forgotten Mr Reddington. She had recaptured, completely and miraculously, that mood of happiness, and in her heart as well as in the world, there was this beauty of promise and of spring.

For weeks there had been a perfect new harmony between herself and Michael; they were friends at last, as well as lovers: she had accepted him as he was and not as she wanted him to be, and she had conquered for good and all, she believed, those black moods of resentment. There remained one forbidden subject, of course, that of Barbara, but in any relationship, she thought, there must be some dangerous ground to be avoided. She had the feeling that her link with Michael was meant and inevitable, and that therefore, somehow, it must be permanent, and all obstacles to its permanency would be removed. In such moods anything was possible; everything was "working together for good" – where had she heard that phrase? She wondered idly. It was as though she had got into the rhythm of life and went with it effortlessly.

Her joy increased and deepened as the day wore on and the time of his arrival drew nearer. The preparation for those few brief hours together was always precious, the buying and cooking of the food he liked, t beautifying of herself and of the flat, and at last the watching for him from a particular window whence she could see the beloved figure as soon as it turned the corner of the square.

But today there was none of the hectic, feverish quality usually present in these preparations. Even though he was late, she experienced none of the old panic. How often had she tortured herself imagining accidents, and knowing that while strangers to her would be notified, his children, his sister, his friends, she who was his love, his wife except in name, would be left in ignorance. They had no mutual friends, no confidant; she often resented his insistence on such secrecy, but she bowed to it for fear of losing him.

But this evening her mood of exaltation was proof even against that old panic; and when at last she heard the well-known footstep on the stair, her joy was so intense that she ran out into the hallway of the flats to meet him, careless of who might be about to witness their embrace. He too, so cautious and so careful lest Barbara might hear of the affaire, threw caution to the winds tonight, and they clung together, there in the public hall, clung as though each would fall without the support of the other.

It was not until she had released herself, and had taken his hand to lead him into the flat, that she saw, standing shivering beside him, its leash fallen on the floor, a little dog.

"Yes," said Michael, "I've brought a visitor; don't know if I did wrong. He's a bit of a sad case, and well – give me a drink, love, and I'll tell you about him."

The dachshund, tail down, padded after him into the strange room, and sat down at his feet, not exploring the place as dogs will. Clare was sentimental over animals, and for this very reason had never allowed herself to apply to the Ministry of Animal Welfare for permission to keep a pet. She would fret, she knew, about leaving it when she went out, and it would be a distraction from her work.

"He's pitifully thin," she said, sitting down on the hearthrug and holding out her hand to the dog. "And so timid. Is he yours, Michael?"

"Doesn't belong to anyone in particular. A fellow at the office had him, but the family broke up because they had one over the three."

She understood this cryptic remark. The State had banned families of over three children; to have more was a crime. Presumably in this case the parents had been put in a Correction Centre, and their offspring in a State Nursery.

"This fellow was going to have the dog put down," went on Michael. "The best thing, perhaps, for he's got a pedigree as long as your arm, and they're always a trouble to rear. However, I thought we'd hold up the death-warrant till you'd had a look at him; I can't keep him myself as my housekeeper loathes dogs, but – " he grinned at her, not finishing the sentence.

"But you thought I might take him," said Clare, her heart warm with gratitude and pride. "You knew he'd be all right with me."

"He'd be company," said Michael. "Get you outdoors more, darling, and take you out of yourself a bit. However, he'll be a tie and a responsibility, so don't say yes without giving it thought."

But she knew she would say yes. It was inevitable because Michael had brought the dog to her, and it was inevitable because Michael had brought the dog to her, and it was inevitable also because of Dragon himself. That was what she had named him in the first five minutes, for he was exactly like a miniature dragon, she decided, with his short legs and his strong tail, and his long-nailed, turned-out feet. It was all part of the happiness of that day when Dragon of his own accord came sniffing up to her, and then, awkwardly and laboriously, climbed on to her lap. His back was so long that his rear parts had to remain on the floor; he laid his beautifully modelled head, with its long nose and silken ears, against her breast, sighed once, heavily, and went to sleep.

As so often when Michael was with her, she herself could not sleep that night. She would lie hour after hour, listening to Michael muttering and shifting beside her, reflecting how strange it was that he, in waking hours so controlled and clam, should be so uneasy in sleep.

But tonight she welcomed insomnia, for a dear dream had come true. Long ago she had known that for her it was enough that he should be here, not making love, not talking, just lying there withdrawn in sleep. Now, for the first time, she was certain that he felt the same. His heart, and not only his body, belonged to her entirely; they had gone beyond the senses to a union of the very being. The rock which was Barbara had disappeared, and already the harbour lights beckoned them home.

That dawn of happiness was no false one; it was prolonged into next day, and for many days thereafter. A second spring had come; to the stormy, hectic period of passion had succeeded a blessed familiarity, the warmth of something long established, old associations binding them else. It was true, really true, that they were just as content when they sat talking quietly, or taking Dragon for a walk on the Common, or doing a crossword puzzle together, as when they were making love. It was not even disturbing that he made no mention of applying to the Ministry of Divorce; that would come in time, and she was content to

121

wait. Even the old panic when he did not ring when he would, or was late for an appointment, was conquered; she could ask him with real interest about his children; her black moods had vanished as though they had never been.

She and Michael had found a private heaven upon earth.

(iii)

"My poor dear child," said a soft voice beside her. "This happiness you have so touchingly described – it was all in your imagination."

The figure of Mr Reddington swam slowly into focus. She blinked at him, wondering what he was doing here, half of her still back in the days of which she had been talking. His eyes held hers, queerly hypnotic, forcing her to go on with the story, to relive that dreadful, hideous evening which she had tried to bury deep down in her mind, that evening that marked the beginning of the end.

After an especially happy meeting, she had waved to Michael from the window until he was out of sight, he turning back every few yards to wave in return, as he always did. Her heart aglow with the joy of the past few hours, no pang of apprehension had touched her, and she hugged to herself his promise to ring her "about Thursday or Friday".

It was summer, and very hot. She felt even less inclined for work than she usually did nowadays, but fetching her sketching-block, pencils, and a rug, sought a quiet spot on the Common where she and Dragon could spend the day. But the Common was full of young lovers, also seeking secluded spots, and ridiculously she was hurt by the sight of them, arms entwined, or pressed together in the long grass. So she and Michael might have been, had they met earlier; they had wasted all their precious youth.

It was a Tuesday when she had waved to him from the window. On Thursday, one of the loveliest days of that halcyon week of weather, she took Dragon for a short walk and returned to the stifling flat to await the promised 'phone call. It did not come. She was more irritated than worried at first; it was unreasonable of him to have asked her from the beginning not to ring him at his office or his flat. What did it matter whether Barbara did somehow get to know about the relationship? She would have to know when he applied for a divorce.

When Friday passed and he had not rung, irritation began to be mingled with an old anxiety. At the beginning of the affaire there had nagged at the back of her mind the intolerable fear that suddenly he might decide to end it, and not having the courage to tell her so, might do it by simply disappearing from her life, trusting to her pride not to try to contact him – particularly as he had made such contacting difficult.

But that was nonsense now. They were not just in love; they loved each other... Then why did he still delay applying to the Ministry of Divorce? Why did he refrain even from discussing such a step with her?

That weekend was a nightmare. She was not yet desperate enough to defy him by ringing, yet she was so much at his beck and call that she must hang about the flat on the chance of his 'phoning her. Even Dragon became a curse during those nightmare days; intensely sensitive to her moods, he was as restless as his mistress, whining round her, cocking his ears at every sound.

So through that weekend she brooded, her resentment growing steadily, her efforts to control it becoming weaker, fresh causes for it recurring to her with every hour. By Monday night her volatile temperament had experienced a new change of mood, and pure anxiety for him seemed to have conquered resentment. Thus she was when the 'phone rang, and she heard his voice, a little hoarse and dreary:

"Hallo, love."

"Oh Michael! Where *have* you been?"

"Had a spot of trouble." (He always made use of under-statements.) "They rang me on Thursday from the Home to say that Barbara had a very bad dose of 'flu and they feared pneumonia. So of course I had to go down."

She dared not speak lest she should ask an unforgivable question.

"She's all right now, thank Brotherhood," he went on, "and I got back last night. Now the only thing I want is to see you. Can I come round tomorrow?"

Almost as soon as she had put the 'phone down, reaction set in. The relief of having heard from him at last, the knowledge that he was all right, and that he still loved her, was succeeded by the bitterest attack of resentment she had ever experienced.

He could have telephoned before. He knew perfectly well how she worried; and if he had not enough imagination to see how impossible a situation it was for her, without her being able to contact him, then he must be made to see it. But the cause of her bitterness lay deeper. "Thank Brotherhood," he had said about Barbara's recovery...

Some small inner voice cried urgently to her: It is dangerous to think on these lines. His concern for his wife was only decent; you know perfectly well that it is you he loves. He has rung, he is coming to see you, it is the only thing he wants. Concentrate on the positive; don't lay yourself open to the pain of a quarrel.

But the blackness had her in its grip, and the small inner voice was choked.

124

It had seemed to her often before that Michael got the vibration of her moods over the telephone, even when she tried to disguise them. Evidently this had happened now, for he came in diffidently, unsure of his reception, and began at once, as though to forestall criticism, on what a Hebrides of a time he had had. He had missed seeing his children, and the Mental Home always gave him the willies.

"But now I feel on top of the world again, just for seeing you."

"Gin and tonic?" enquired Clare, her voice carefully level.

"I don't want a drink. I want a kiss."

She smiled, as at a child, and lifted her cheek; easily snubbed, he kissed her perfunctorily, sighed, and sat down, beginning to hum a tune under his breath, a sure sign that he was either annoyed or uneasy. Dragon, who loved him dearly, leapt on to his knees and began lavishing upon him the affection which Clare had denied.

"You know, Michael," she said, standing with her arm on the chimney-shelf, looking down into her drink, "we simply must come to some other arrangement about getting in touch if something happens. You must see it's not fair to me to have to wait around until you choose to 'phone."

"Rang you as soon as ever I could," he said abruptly. "We've been into all this before, and we've agreed that it's one of the penalties of the relationship. We've been very lucky, seeing each other as often as we have."

"You talk as though we were living in sin, as they used to call it."

"Well, I don't know what they call it nowadays," said Michael carelessly, "but it comes to the same thing."

"Michael – "

"Look, darling, I'm tired and nervy, and I came here hoping for some peace and quiet. For Man's sake don't let's have a row."

"I had not the slightest intention of having a row," she replied, her hand shaking so much that she was obliged to put down her glass. "I asked you something perfectly reasonable, and all I get is self-pity."

He grinned unpleasantly.

"Self-pity. Pot calling kettle black, eh?"

"I must go and get dinner," said Clare, and walked out of the room.

It was a horribly constrained meal. Clare realized during it what she ought to have realized before, that Michael was considerably drunk when he came to the flat. She knew the symptoms, and she had experience of the way drink affected him; ordinarily sweet-tempered and equable, he became touchy, almost sadistic, and there was only one safe way of dealing with him, to keep things strictly on the surface. Instead, drinking too much herself, she grew more and more emotional, more and more determined to have a show-down. It appeared to her vitally important that, once and for all, they sorted out the situation; and by the time dinner was ended, it was the whole relationship, and not just the fact of being unable to get in touch with him in emergencies, that she was determined to sort out.

But for a while he gave her no chance. His overpowering sexual desire for her awoke her own passion, yet in the midst of love-making she was aware of the absence of tenderness on his part, and this put the finishing touch to her misery. At first, seeing her tears, he was kind and anxious, but as they continued he grew irritated, and presently, getting up, he dressed in silence and went into the sitting-room. She put on a wrap and followed, to find him pouring himself another drink. She had reached a familiar stage in the quarrel now; alcohol and emotion had combined to blur her memory, so that she could not be sure what she had said. Certain only that it could not be forgiven or taken back, perversely, having gone so far, she felt the urge to plunge deeper and make it worse.

"Well," she said, fumbling for a cigarette, "now that you've had what you came for, I suppose you want to go home."

"Reckon it would have been better if I hadn't come," he growled, flinging himself into a chair. He took a gulp of gin and tonic. "Might have known I'd find you in one of your tantrums. But after such a Hebrides of a weekend, I just wanted you, tantrums and all."

"Everything is what *you* want, isn't it?"

He gave that unpleasant grin again.

"My dear girl, if ever there was a completely selfish little bitch, its name is Clare Bentley."

"Not like Barbara, I suppose?"

"No, not like Barbara," he said, his voice as cold as the strokes of a hammer.

She looked at him. She tried to speak incisively, but her voice shook like a harpstring.

"Once and for all, Michael, when are you going to the Ministry of Divorce?"

"Once and for all, Clare, I'm not going – ever."

She knew then, irrevocably, in one blinding, searing flash, that all her new-found happiness was delusion, that his heart belonged to his mad wife.

"Get out!" she screamed. "Get out, or I'll… "

"If I had had a knife, I would have killed him," she said. "I would! And yet it wasn't I. It was some horrible alien thing that had taken possession of me, that lusted to hurt and kill, something I couldn't conquer, some devil – "

"Come, my dear child, you know there are no such things as devils," said the soothing voice of Mr

Reddington. "Of course it was you, and you had every justification for feeling as you did. But soon there will be nothing of you left to be so tormented. There will be only Peace Unlimited."

(iv)

She stared at him dazedly, still living in that other world, exhausted by the blackness which still raged somewhere in her mind. Then gradually the sense of his last words drove itself home to her, and again, and more strongly than ever before, her whole being yearned for oblivion.

"I would like to know exactly what the procedure is," she said abruptly. "It's not that I'm afraid; indeed I wish I had not to wait so long. Please don't think – "

"My dear!" He was almost uncannily quick on the uptake, was Mr Reddington, F.E.R.S., and apparently had no difficulty in understanding her curt demand. "People who are afraid don't want to know. I am glad you have asked me that, Clare; it is what I should have expected of you. You want to face it all boldly and realistically. If you will allow me, I will take you to see our Temple of Rest."

Clare had not bargained for that.

"But," she faltered, "do you mean that we can't – well, go out – in privacy, in our own room?"

"In privacy, of course," replied Mr Reddington, very solemn. "But you will understand, my dear, that for practical reasons, and for the sake of our other guests, it is best to have a chamber set apart."

She felt suddenly nauseated, but pride forbade her to demur, as Mr Reddington hastened to open the door for her, gesturing to the right along the passage.

It was very strange indeed to pass white-coated waiters in the corridor, and to hear the cheerful clatter of pots and pans from the kitchen; a marmalade cat was curled up in the sun on a chair. (Dragon barked challengingly at the cat, which opened its amber eyes and closed them again in contempt.) In little over a week, reflected Clare, I shall be coming this way again, and it will be my last walk. Other people will be reading the papers or watching television or playing bridge, and there in the kitchens they will be preparing an elaborate meal.

She remembered the stories she had heard in her childhood of criminals going to their execution, the clock striking eight, the tray of breakfast things in the condemned cell (the victim could choose what he liked to eat, she believed, on that last morning), the grim little procession, the prison Governor, the sheriff, the hangman, the chaplain, the ritual shaking of hands before those hands were strapped, the short walk to the shed with its hideous apparatus. How could any man – or woman, for they had hanged women sometimes – have endured it? How really much more merciful and civilized the world had become. Yes, she must concentrate on that thought...

"Do I come alone when – when it happens?" she asked in a small voice.

He was striding along ahead of her, vigorous, healthy, but he paused at once, and took her arm.

"It is for our martyrs to choose, Clare. Some prefer complete privacy; other find a certain consolation in having Mrs Reddington or myself with them."

"But somebody has to be there to – to do it."

His arm stiffened in hers.

"Clare!" His voice was gently reproachful. "You cannot think what you are saying. This is *self*-elimination, my dear, not State-elimination. We are here only to assist, to make everything easy – "

"But surely," she cried, not knowing that she interrupted, "at the last moment some people must – well, get cold feet."

He shook his head with smiling complacence.

"No, my dear Clare, we have never had that tragedy. Human nature is weak as yet, we know, or rather I should say that the instinct of self-preservation, left over from the bad old days when Man had fight for his existence, is strong, and that is precisely why our beloved Prime Minister insisted that there should be two weeks spent in a Home of Rest before self-elimination. Our martyrs must be allowed time to prepare themselves for the great sacrifice; they must (forgive me) keep as it were a vigil like some squire of old before he received the honour of knighthood, assisted by those who, like myself, are trained for this work. I do not like to appear to boast, but I must tell you that I have had such extraordinary success in helping our martyrs in their physical and mental orientation, that not one, *not one*, Clare, has shrunk from his noble act."

She remembered suddenly that torn scrap of paper she had found inside her wardrobe on the evening of her arrival, the four words in the shaky hand, "Dear God, forgive me." But before she could pursue the conversation, she saw that they had arrived. He unlocked a green baize door marked "Private," and she found herself in a sort of anteroom, pleasant but characterless. Crossing this, her guide unlocked an inner door, threw it open, and with a gesture of apology preceded her into what she still thought of, perversely, as the execution-shed.

She stood on the threshold, gathering impressions.

The first thing that struck her was that while there were no windows, the room appeared to be full of sunlight; then she realized that this soft primrose glow, resembling a wood in spring, must come from cunningly concealed lighting. There was no hint of stuffiness, for the room was air-conditioned, nor was there anything which could cause claustrophobia, for besides the fact that the apartment was of a fair size, the walls were painted to give the effect of vistas.

Like everywhere else at Fremley Manor, the Temple of Rest was spotlessly clean and furnished with a faintly old-fashioned touch which was both restful and homely. The colour scheme was dove-grey with touches of white; there were plenty of fresh flowers from the greenhouses, yet not so many as even remotely to suggest a funeral; and except for absence of magazines, the room might have been a hotel lounge. There were even ashtrays, and most incongruous of all, a radiogram. She had forgotten Mr Reddington, but evidently he had not forgotten her; as her glance lingered on this latter object, he stepped quietly across and turned a switch. Immediately the triumphant and really moving strains of the Martyrs' Hymn issued from the cabinet.

"It is our last tribute to our beloved guests," he murmured with emotion. "But I must tell you that if they make a request for some other record, we have a wide choice at their disposal. Yet somehow, if I may take an example from the bad old days when there was war, we find that there is one particular piece of music which seems most apt to express this new tenet of our faith, just as the Last Post was considered most suitable for military funerals. So usually we have the Martyrs' Hymn."

He switched off the radiogram.

"And now, my dear Clare, you have seen our Temple of Rest where you will make the supreme sacrifice and win the reward of oblivion. Does if offend you?"

In this room, she thought, this very morning, at least one person has killed himself, "committed suicide," as they used to say. And every day the same thing happens...but what does happen?

"How is it done?" she asked, aware of the crudeness of the question, but unable to frame it any other way.

"The martyr orders what he or she wishes to drink," replied Mr Reddington, quite natural and at ease. "Tea, coffee, or perhaps something the teeniest bit stronger," he added with an arch smile. "And that is all. You know what the word 'euthanasia' means, my dear. Gentle and easy death. I can assure you that it is. There is no fraction of pain or even of discomfort; we are in a position to assert this positively, for our doctors have been able to discover, by an examination of the nervous system after death, that there has been no suffering. You know that for years we have experimented on the incurably sick and the insane. This fact is of especial comfort to me, Clare, in the case of self-elimination, for our martyrs have suffered so cruelly in their minds, that I could not bear that there should be even an instant of physical pain when they come to make their supreme sacrifice."

"And then what happens?" demanded Clare, refusing to be drawn into a discussion beyond sordid details.

He looked a little hurt.

"Why trouble your beautiful head about that?" he asked gently. "But if you really desire to know, it is the same as our disposal of all unwanted matter nowadays. Cleanly and in a few seconds, the body is reduced to dust, which itself rapidly disintegrates until there is nothing left at all. I am no scientist, so that I cannot explain it in its proper terms, but the great marvel is that this particular atomic pencil destroys only flesh and bones and the rest of the constituents of the human body; the inanimate objects in the vicinity remain unaffected. We have reached the point when we can abolish only that which we desire to abolish – "

"Except unhappiness. We destroy the rose, maybe, and leave the thorn."

It was his silence, prolonged and significant, that made her realize what she had said. She glanced at him, and now he did not look like an old-fashioned host, a family doctor, or a kindly priest. The hearty manner, the cosy smile, the understanding look, were gone; and just for an instant, so fleeting that afterwards she was sure she had imagined it, something sly and almost evil peeped out from his eyes. Then he was beside her, and had taken her hands.

"You are too sensitive, my dear Clare. It was a mistake after all to have brought you to this room. Come back to my den and – "

"We have perfected destruction," she insisted, "but we are farther than ever from creating happiness."

"We have created at all the means of happiness, my dear child," said Mr Reddington, very grave and priest-like now. "Material security, health, freedom from war, wealth and comfort, ever increasing freedom from pain. This happiness of which you speak is, I assure you, imaginary – "

He broke off with a sharp exclamation, as from behind him there came suddenly a long-drawn, eerie howl.

For the first time then, Clare became aware of Dragon. He sat pressed against the door, his muzzle pointing towards the ceiling, and again as she looked he gave that primitive, spine-chilling howl. She ran to him, murmuring endearments, all else forgotten; but then came the final horror. His hackles up, foam on his lips, he shrank from her; gentlest and most affectionate of beasts, he even showed his teeth when she bent to pick him up.

Clare drew back aghast, and as a hand opened the door, Dragon whisked through the opening, down the corridor, and up the stairs.

Chapter Eight

(i)

"I've been looking for you everywhere," Clare whispered. "Where have you been?"

"Getting on with the good work," replied Stephen, regarding her curiously as she stood in the open doorway of her room. "Never an idle moment here, y'know. Want me?"

"Yes, I do. Please come in and shut the door."

"Can't it wait? I'm not in what you might call a sympathetic mood at the moment – "

"It's not about me. There's something wrong with Dragon."

He came instantly into the room at that.

"He's crouching there under the eiderdown," said Clare, shutting the door. "He won't let me touch him; he even – he even snapped at me."

Stephen went straight to the bed, sat down on it, and began to talk softly and soothingly to the small mound under the covers. After a few minutes the eiderdown was agitated by the slight waving of a tail; Stephen reached under and took the dog into his arms. Dragon whined and shivered, his eyes slanting towards his mistress, but he allowed himself to be picked up by the man and nursed in the armchair, his whines gradually ceasing.

134

"What happened?" demanded Stephen, gently tickling the dog's stomach.

"I asked to be shown the – the Temple of Rest. I'd no idea it would upset – "

"You bloody little fool!" furiously shouted Stephen. "How dare you take Dragon there!"

She recoiled from his anger, and her pale face grew whiter still.

"But he will have to go there when I go finally."

"He'll be given dope then. You're a devil for punishment, Clare, the complete masochist, but you might have refrained from taking Dragon to a place where he at least would never go willingly for what's done there. Don't you know *anything* about dogs? Don't you know how sensitive they are to atmosphere? You're not fit to be trusted with the care of anything, even an animal."

He relented little at the misery in her eyes.

"Do with a drink, both of us," said he, reaching into a pocket. "Always carry something on my hip. Go on, go on, it isn't doped. So you've been with the Lord High, have you?"

"Yes. And he made me say things – things I've never told anybody. Stephen, does he experiment on people here? On their minds, I mean?"

"The penny has dropped at last," observed Stephen, slopping whisky into a tumble. "My dear girl, be your age. You don't mean to tell me you were taken in by all that guff of APS's about giving her blessed martyrs two weeks of bliss before they popped themselves off?"

"You mean – that's why we're given these two weeks? So that sadistic brutes like Reddington can torture us – "

I've never met anyone like you for manufacturing horrors," Stephen interrupted with a humorous sigh. "The Lord High's interested in euthanasia. Well, that's fairly obvious from the letters after his name, isn't it? You can't blame him for wanting to find out the exact amount of dope needed for individual cases. And why this sudden objection to experimenting? You don't object to it when it's the insane or the incurably ill who are the guinea-pigs. It simply hurts your colossal vanity. Clare Bentley, S A, vivisected!"

"It may be just my vanity. I don't know. Stephen, isn't it possible to forgo these fourteen days? Don't they ever make exceptions?"

"No, never. You can't escape like that, you know."

Escape. Words jumped into her mind – "Fear wist not to evade, as Love wist to pursue." She must be going mad.

Stephen regarded her with his head on one side.

"You know," he said, "I sometimes think there must be something in what the Christians call Original Sin. For we're so unreasonable in our vices. You, for instance, make no secret of the fact that you dislike me, yet because I didn't go wild with delight when you invited me into your room just now, you were thoroughly peeved."

She said nothing. She sat limply on the side of her bed, her face pinched with exhaustion. Still regarding her covertly, Stephen went on:

"Then take Margaret. She played merry Hebrides this morning because she'd ordered a new bottle of nail varnish from the Beauty Parlour, and they gave her something called 'Provocative Pink' when she had distinctly ordered 'Alluring Pink'. Without a strong magnifying-glass, no one could tell the difference, but apparently my lady wouldn't be seen dead in Provocative Pink. And that's what's so perverse. She's due to go tomorrow, and she certainly won't be 'seen dead' in Provocative Pink or in any other colour. She'll be a handful of dust in a minute, and not even that in another eight and a half."

There was silence. Then Clare said abruptly:

"I want to ask you a favour. When I go, will you have Dragon?"

Without answering her, he mused:

"You've changed quite a bit since you came here, y'know. You've even got to the point of being human enough to think of something else besides yourself. Yes, in spite of what I said a while back. Go on; hit me."

"Please have Dragon. What you said a while back was quite true. I betrayed him; I'm not fit to be trusted with an animal. Dragon likes you; he's only six, and really quite healthy. It wouldn't be fair to take him again, doped or not, to that ghastly room with the Martyrs' Hymn booming out from the radiogram, and ashtrays, and – and everything."

"Why the Hebrides did you let the Lord High take you there on a conducted tour? You certainly are a glutton for punishment. But about Dragon, I don't know. My own plans are a bit uncertain."

She stared at him in dismay.

"You've got the sack? Through me, too. The Lord High realized that you're not giving me my proper ration of dope and he's – "

"Oh Brotherhood!" groaned Stephen. "How you women always must be the centre of everything! It's got nothing to do with you, and I haven't got the sack. It's simply that I'm thinking of applying for another sort of job. I'm disgusted, fed up to the teeth, or, if you like, just can't take it."

He replaced the now sleeping Dragon under the eiderdown, and began to prowl about the room.

"There was Felicity this morning. Remember the lady who looked like a picture of the front row of the chorus in some old musical? She went so gallantly; she put on a costume from some show donkeys' years old. But not because she wanted to be theatrical. That's me, she seemed to say. That's me, and I failed, but that's how I would have liked to have succeeded. And, 'I'm sorry, darling', she said to me in a stage whisper, 'to give you all this trouble.' (She'd asked for some ancient record we hadn't got.) She had her little audience, the Lord High, and the Lady High, and me, and off she went, with her cheap perfume and her greenroom air, making her exit, a trouper to the last. And believing to the last, bless her warm heart, that she'd meet all the boys and girls again, somewhere back-stage. Perhaps she has. I hope she has," he added defiantly. And then, with a return to his sardonic air: "See what I mean about it being impossible for me to stay on at Fremley?"

"But even if you left, you could still have Dragon."

"A one-track mind, has Miss Clare Bentley. Look, girl, Dragon went a bit loco because you were fool enough to take him into that room. He's perfectly all right now, and you're going to need him; you've over a week to go yet, and if I did consent to take him, it would be now."

He watched her curiously as he spoke, and he saw the instant struggle in her mind. He hit harder.

"You won't see him again if I take him. It wouldn't be fair on the dog. I should keep him down at the Lodge where I live. You'll have a week without a friend of any sort, and so far as I am concerned, without your proper dope. You may think you're gutsy, but I doubt if anyone's gutsy enough to stand a week like that at Cowards' Hall."

"I can't explain," Clare said in a voice scarcely audible. "I'm all muddled inside myself. Only I want Dragon to be happy."

"And how do you know he'll be happy with me? Don't tell me you trust me."

She got off the bed, went uncertainly to the window, and stood there with her back turned.

"One has to trust someone." She turned that over in her mind, as though she had made a surprising discovery. "Please take the dog, Stephen, now this minute. You were right from the beginning; I'm so gutless I can't even say goodbye to him."

He said nothing. He picked up Dragon and went quickly out of the room.

(ii)

The moon shone full into Clare's window that night. She sat staring at it after she had prepared for bed, and through her mind, drained and exhausted, streamed disconnected thoughts. Yet presently she perceived that they were not entirely disconnected; there seemed to be an underlying theme.

Richard, the scientist, looking for some pattern in the story; Mrs Smith talking about being a steward for her pathetic bits and pieces of furniture, loving to polish and care for them for someone else, asking only to be needed. Felicity who couldn't get around to thinking that her pals weren't somewhere any longer; Stephen, even Stephen, saying that he hoped she was right.

A hunger in so many diverse types, a hunger for something explained away by the psychologists. So many eliminating themselves, more and more according to Stephen, simply because they had this yearning which a material utopia could not satisfy. Was not that a sort of proof that man was not meant to find paradise on earth?

And Linda. Linda was in danger. If only I could get a message through to her, she thought; and instantly, as though an actual voice had spoken, her mind said, "Do you think she'd want to come away?" She is very well. She is very happy. So Peter had said. So she had been in that queer dream. Stephen, too, had spoken of what he called joy when recounting his forced landing in the Hebrides. And now the State was thinking of wiping out these odd cranks in the reservations, because few though they were and surely harmless, the State feared them. "They would like to despise us, to ignore us, but it seems they can't."

Peter. A pretty poor example of Christian. By his own confession it had only taken five months for him to succumb to the pagan atmosphere he had found on his return to civilization. All that silly talk about cutting the telephone wires between himself and his Creator; it just didn't make sense. A wretched specimen he was, feeble, servile, slightly theatrical, starting out to convert the progressives, and in five months glad enough of the chance to "commit suicide," as he would call it. She felt a dull fury against him; she had really wanted to know what defence he could put up for his ridiculous beliefs, but he was only the blind leading the blind, staving her off with empty words, grovelling about his own failure, whining to the State, his sworn enemy, for a gentle and easy death...

Then her mood changed, and she was pricked by remorse. She had been abominably rude to him, and not a little cruel. She had a vision of him stumbling away over the tree roots, the embodiment of despair. He was as vulnerable as Dragon, as though weak, she had sensed in him a kind of bitter sincerity. Could she go and apologize to him? She would like to say – well, just that she was sorry to have been unkind. After all, they were both in the same boat now, and who was she to judge him?

He was there, next door to her, sleeping under a mercy drug. At least, she thought suddenly, though he's certainly next door, he doesn't appear to be sleeping. She realized now that for some while past she had been aware of sounds of movement in the room next door, and that now there were strange shadows on the bay window which jutted out beyond her own, busy, restless shadows thrown by the moon, through the night was still and no branch moved.

She became interested, vaguely disquieted, though she could not tell why. Had Peter, like herself, refused to be doped, and was he walking restlessly up and down? She would almost have said dancing up and down, those shadows were so strange and jerky.

Listening, straining her ears, she heard what seemed to be the dragging about of furniture, and then a groan, instantly stifled. He's trying to escape, she thought; perhaps they've locked him in, and he's trying to get down from the window.

Don't be such a dramatic fool, she rebuked herself. And what does it matter to you what he's doing? Go to bed; drink your doped milk; get through the night somehow. Tell Stephen tomorrow that you've changed your mind, and that you'll have your proper ration of the drug in future. And ask him to give you Dragon back. You simply haven't the guts to go through the rest of the time without...

All was quiet now next door. But it was sinister quietness. For still the moonlight threw a shadow on the window, a queer black shadow that swung to and fro, up in the air, where no shadow should be...

She felt sick from the rapid beating of her heart. Something was wrong, hideously wrong in that room next door. I must get on to the house 'phone, she thought; I must call for help. But she seemed paralysed, and wondered for a moment whether all this were not a nightmare, or perhaps the effect of an accumulation of drugs.

Yet she knew it was neither. She felt cold and calm and wide-awake. A strong impulsion seized on her to go into that room next door, to see for herself the horror there. And with the impulsion was a curious conviction that somehow all this was intended, even to its last detail, that this was why she had given Dragon away this evening, even why she had come to the Home of Rest...

She got up from the window-seat, deliberately, fastened her robe more securely round her, stood just for a moment like a swimmer on the brink of a racing tide, then tiptoed out of the room. The handle of Peter's door turned at her touch; it was not locked. She opened the door cautiously, whispering his name; but the word froze on her lips.

There was no need to switch on the light. The moon lit that grim scene all too plainly. The slight figure hanging by its neck from the ring that held the electric fixture, slowly turning on a length of cord. The gashes inexpertly dug in hands and bare feet, and the blood dripping from them, noiseless and slow, on to the deep-pile carpet.

PART TWO

Chapter One

"The ambulance will be here directly," repeated Mr Reddington, padding about Clare's bedroom in old-fashioned carpet slippers. He had said it at least six times already.

"You are sure he's going to live?" whispered Clare.

"By your own prompt action, my dear, in summoning aid, he is going to live, and he is going to pay for his disgusting behaviour. That the wretch should have chosen Fremley for it!" raged Mr Reddington. "The best run Home of Rest in Britain!"

"I do *hope* dear Enid hasn't seen anything," twittered his wife. "She goes tomorrow morning – I mean, of course, it is tomorrow morning now – and you know how she does detest any uncleanness. If she saw that blood!" Mrs Reddington gave a shudder. "And all over my beautiful carpet too!"

"Don't you think Clare ought to get some sleep?" enquired Stephen.

The Reddingtons said in chorus, Yes, yes, poor dear Clare must certainly get some sleep after her frightful ordeal, and have a little something to quieten her nerves. But they said it half-heartedly. Unacquainted with death except under his polite alias, euthanasia, they had changed as completely as if a mask had slipped form them. Gone the doctor-host, the lady from an expensive store's advertisement; they were partly outraged Man, and partly two Government employees who, through no fault of their own, might find themselves in trouble with the Ministry of Self-Elimination. Mr Reddington's healthy face was pale, his hair stood up in an absurd quiff, and he looked oddly defenceless without his bow tie. His wife was without make-up, and regrettably had her hair done up in pins.

"I really don't know whether to be relieved or not that you were able to revive the brute with artificial respiration, Stephen," stormed Mr Reddington, still packing up and down. "There would have had to be an inquest, of course, if he'd died, but as it is I have been obliged to send for the police. The police at Fremley Manor! Oh no, it really is too much!"

"But why?" asked Clare, feeling an hysterical desire to laugh. "That's what he came here to do – to kill himself, isn't it? Surely that's perfectly legal in a Home of Rest?"

Mr Reddington paused in his pacing and stared at her in outrage.

"Clare," he said, making a valiant effort to control himself, "I realize that you are very upset, which is quite understandable after such a shock. But I really must ask you not to use such improper terms. The man called Peter came here to self-eliminate, and only under the conditions laid down in the Act. He broke the rule whereby self-eliminators must spend two weeks in a Home of Rest; people can't die just when they feel like it, my dear; it is for the State to tell them when. What he did was a disgusting crime, or at least a very serious misdemeanour – trying to *hang* himself! And apart from that, he entered Fremley under false pretences, feigning to be one of our dear martyrs, sacrificing himself for the common good."

"Oh no, it wasn't like that at all," said Clare.

"I blame the Board of Investigation," Mr Reddington swept on, paying no heed to this remark. "They should have discovered that this Peter was quite ineligible for self-elimination, and that he was not, as he pretended, converted from his preposterous beliefs. When we – er – cut him down, we found he was wearing a crucifix; and on a chain too," raged Mr Reddington, as though that somehow made it worse.

He was like a fanatically house-proud lady who has discovered bugs in her drawing room.

"Oh *dear!*" wailed Mrs Reddington.

"I am sorry, Freda, to harrow you with these details, but really we have to face facts. And yet how typical it all is of these Christians! Sneaking about in disguise, as they have done throughout the ages, taking pride in upsetting other people, showing off, never happy unless they are making others miserable, actually loving detestable things like pain. Not content with trying to hang himself, the wretch must go and dig holes in his hands and feet. I have always been somewhat against this new move to eliminate the Christians with a mercy bomb, but after this, such an act would have my whole-hearted approval. To come to Fremley of all places with deliberate intent to kill himself – "

"But that's why we all come to Fremley," squealed Clare, hugging herself and shivering. "That's why Fremley exists. Oh it's so funny – so funny – "

Mrs Reddington swooped on her.

"Now, sweetheart, you positively must get some rest. I am afraid, dear, that you will not now be left in the peace which is your right. There will be nasty questions, darling; I mean by the police. Naturally they will need to probe the whole horrible business, and you see it was you who found this brute. But I am sure it won't interfere with your own elimination; most happily you have more than a week left of your fortnight, and perhaps we could persuade the authorities to make an exception and extend the time. Fred, do go and get dressed; there is the ambulance bell," she added, agitatedly hustling her husband out of the room.

Stephen shut the door behind the Reddingtons, and said sharply:

"Clare, be careful."

"What?"

"You're saying things you don't mean, things that might be dangerous."

"I'm not sure that I don't mean them."

"Even more dangerous, you silly bitch," snapped Stephen. "I don't know what this man Peter has been saying to you, but you've changed ever since he came here. If you go defending him, you may find yourself accused as an accessory."

She began to laugh painfully again, huddled in the armchair.

"It sounds so silly, so fantastic! 'An accessory after the fact' – isn't that the jargon? You'd think he'd committed a murder, when all he did was what everyone else has come here precisely to do, only in his own way."

She put her hand across her mouth and gabbled through it:

"His own way. Why did he do it like that, Stephen? He'd taken such – such trouble. He'd pinched a knife from the dining-room, and jabbed it through his hands and feet. He made it all into a sort of ritual. It was a though he wanted to – to make some sort of amends to someone."

"Perhaps he did."

"Oh I wish he'd died! It seems so awful that he should be dragged back to life after he'd gone to all that trouble. He was so wretchedly unhappy, and I was so mean to him.

And now he's back in the hands of the State again, and he'll be tormented with questions – "

"Perhaps that's the sort of amends he's required to make."

She looked at him a moment, shook her head in bewilderment, and asked in a small, strained voice:

"Can I have Dragon back?"

"No."

"Where is he?"

"Down at the Lodge where I live. Perfectly happy learning to be a dog. He hasn't howled once, and he drinks plain water without honey and likes it; he gnaws bones and they don't stick in his throat."

She nodded. She felt that queer light-headedness which comes from shock or exhaustion. She began to talk, but more to herself than to Stephen.

"On the floor in Peter's room, lying at his feet, there was a little book. It had blood on it, but I picked it up and put it into the pocket of my gown before I called you and the Reddingtons. And do you know, inside it, marking a place, was a poem written out very small. It was *The Hound of Heaven*. It was almost as though Peter had left it there hoping I should find it, because he had been quoting that poem to me the first time we talked."

"You're laying up a packet of trouble for yourself, my girl," remarked Stephen.

"The book was the old New Testament, I mean the Christian one," Clare continued, paying no attention, "and while you were all next door attending to Peter, I glanced through it. It's the strangest thing! It's like something written in cipher which doesn't make sense unless you have the key. I don't suppose I have, and yet bits of it did make me think. There was something about the two great Commandments, loving God first and then your neighbour; we've not so much reversed them as cut the first one out. We've made it our prime duty to love Man in the abstract; but does Man love us?"

"Did the Christian God?"

"Oh yes. That was the whole essence of the thing. And don't begin about 'then why does He permit pain?', because it's an old one, and quite irrelevant."

"I don't see why."

"Nor do I really, except that you can't have love without pain. I know that. Everyone knows it if they've ever really loved. But I ask you, can you honestly love Man in the abstract?"

"The answer is no."

"Well then!"

"Look, Clare, you'd better get to bed and try for some sleep. I haven't the least idea what you're getting at."

"Not unreasonable," she said with a small smile, "because I haven't much idea myself. I'm sort of groping. No, wait, Stephen; it's terribly important. You said yourself that in spite of all we've got materially, most people are unhappy. They still lack something, something essential. And all we can offer them is a vague, impersonal abstraction we call Humanity, which nobody can honestly say they love, and which we've agreed can't love us."

He looked at her, thoughtfully.

"I don't get it," he said. "Surely of all people this man called Peter is the last to make you think along these anti-Brotherhood lines. A more wretched specimen of a Christian I have yet to meet. He committed, or tried to commit, the ultimate sin. They at least still believe in suicide."

"But he did it because he was sorry, I mean he did it that way. You yourself suggested that he wanted to make amends. Well, don't you see that he could have gone the easy way we're all going, the tasteless poison in the cup of tea? But though he'd lost his beliefs, as he said through his own fault, he'd still try to make some sort of fantastic reparation to someone in whom he still *wanted* to believe. It was a kind of desperate act of – well, repentance. It was as though he said, 'I've failed you, but at least I'll try to be like you at the end, and perhaps that will make up a little'. For he tried in his poor clumsy way to crucify himself – "

"I've warned you," Stephen interrupted harshly. "If you babble this sort of dangerous nonsense to anyone else, you're in for a packet of trouble, my girl."

He turned and stalked out of the room.

(ii)

She slept, and woke. Her body ached as though she had gone through some physical ordeal, and her mind still churned over the chaotic ideas which had come to her during the night.

It was afternoon now; a tray of lunch simmered on a hot-point beside her bed, but she could not face food. She wanted to be by herself in the open air. The day was mild and sweet, and when she had dressed she wandered down into the gardens, avoiding the other "guests," sitting down presently under a great monkey-puzzler on the lower lawn. Its armoured tentacles made a screen, dangling above her like elongated artichokes.

But she was not destined to be alone for long. Across the lawn there approached a stranger, a middle-aged gentleman in a dark town suit and bowler hat, carrying a briefcase. He came purposefully into her exotic green tent, and her heart sank.

"You must forgive this intrusion, Miss Bentley," said he, raising his hat. "Are you feeling rested enough to talk?"

"Oh yes, thank you. Are you a – a police officer?"

He smiled reassuringly.

"No, indeed. I am a doctor. Our good friend, Mr Reddington, asked me to have a word with you, as naturally he was anxious about you after such a shock. May I sit down?"

Receiving permission, he sat down beside her, laying his briefcase on the other side of the seat, and opening it to disclose a pile of papers. He began to question her gently. They were the kind of questions a doctor would ask, and he seemed an extraordinarily understanding physician. So much so that she did not feel alarmed when presently the conversation took a rather unusual turn.

"Miss Bentley, you have passed through an ordeal which, I can assure you, is quite unique for one in your circumstances. You must believe me, therefore, when I say that it would be entirely reasonable if it had caused you to have second thoughts about the purpose which brought you here to Fremley."

"I don't quite see what you mean," she said in mild astonishment.

"Please do not misunderstand me. I am perfectly acquainted with all the facts of your sad case, and had I been a member of the Board of Investigation which permitted you to come here, I must certainly have concurred in their verdict. But from what Mr Reddington tells me, I have wondered whether your state of mind is quite what it was. I will not go into technical details, but the result of shock is often very strange and unexpected. And, Miss Bentley, the last thing which our good kind mother, the State, desires is that any of her children should eliminate themselves if there is some cure for their malady. Let me add something personal, if you will not think me impertinent. No one would be happier than I if, after all, we were not to lose one of our favourites State Artists."

"Do you mean – I could leave Fremley?"

He smiled again.

"Ah, I see you want to. I wonder, is it because, while you have been here, you have begun to realize that you (forgive me) were in such mortal pain that you forgot someone else very deeply concerned in your welfare?"

She was silent, her head spinning. She was perfectly aware that by "someone else" he meant Michael Standish. She was equally aware, with a shame-faced shock, that for the past forty-eight hours she had not once thought about Michael. For five years he had never been absent from her mind all her waking hours; he had intruded into her dreams; he had been an obsession from which, latterly, she should have prayed to be delivered, had she believed in prayer.

"You are aware, no doubt," went on the grave professional voice beside her, "that the whereabouts of those who choose to enter our Homes of Rest are kept secret even from their nearest and dearest. We have to be cruel to be kind. But did you really suppose, my dear Miss Bentley, that this – ah – gentleman would not guess what had happened and make every effort to find you? I am afraid you are too modest, and perhaps you were a little precipitate in applying for self-elimination. And yet I think it is possible that there will be a happy ending after all to your romance. It may well be that your desperate decision opened the eyes of this – ah – gentleman, and showed him where his true happiness was to be found."

She was not listening; she was absorbed in a discovery. I am myself again, she thought; the bond is loosed; I am released from the treadmill. I don't know yet whether I love Michael still, or whether that precious, fragile thing was destroyed by all their psycho-analysing. It might even be that I never really loved him, that it was just what is termed infatuation. I only know that I can look at him objectively at last, see him as a person in his own right, and not just as someone necessary to my happiness. I can see him as having a life of his own, apart from me; he isn't just Michael-and-Clare; he is Michael. Other people love and need him; his children; Barbara...

She heard herself say, but as though it were someone else speaking with her voice:

"Yes, I would like to leave Fremley."

"I am so very glad, my dear Miss Bentley, to hear you say that. For it means that your whole case can be reopened."

When he had left her, Clare began to walk. Some sort of physical exercise was necessary to reassure her that at least her body still belonged to her. Her mind had become fluid; it could not cope with all the indigestible ideas which had crowded into it during the past twelve hours. I am free, she told herself, trying to clutch at facts; suddenly, as by a miracle, I am free. My soul is delivered like a bird out of the net of the fowler – wherever have I heard that strange phrase before? I am free to go back into the world out of this house of death; I need never go into that sinister room with the ashtrays and the radiogram and the soft and evil primrose light. And perhaps, though not certainly, I am free from the Michael obsession...

But do I really want to go back, even if I could begin again where I was before ever I met Michael?

Something warned her that she would never be the old Clare. If it were true that Michael had gone from her heart, then a part of her had died with his going. And if he had not gone? Could she, now, recapture the old ecstasy? She was maddened by this perverse creature who was herself. One moment coming to a decision, the next questioning the wisdom of it. Fragments of what the doctor had said returned to her; Michael had been frantic about her, had made every effort to find her. What she had done had brought him to his senses; she was having everything handed to her on a plate, and yet here she was, doubting her own feelings, belatedly deciding to leave the field clear for Barbara. What is Barbara to me, she demanded, except a hated rival?

She became suddenly conscious of her surroundings. Over a low, neatly clipped hedge, she could see the garden of the Lodge, and a familiar brown figure in it. Mouth open, silky ears blown back by the wind of his haste, Dragon was racing round and round in circles, taking the corners as it were on to wheels; the embodiment of joyous doghood.

Nothing remains, she thought, all passes, even the love of a little dog. What Stephen told me about Dragon is true; he's perfectly happy. And as for Michael, one cannot recapture the past. If I go back into the world again, I shall go completely alone; I shan't even be the same Clare who came to Fremley. I've got all muddled up inside myself. A new life to live; so many readjustments to make; no, definitely I can't face it. Better the Man you know than the God you don't know...

I'll have a word with Mr Reddington this evening, and tell him that in spite of what I said to the doctor, I still want to stub out the last cigarette in the ashtray and drink the last drink in his Temple of Rest.

(iii)

She sat on the window-seat in her room, reading *The Hound of Heaven*. It no longer alarmed her; it was pleasantly wistful. Like reading about a shipwreck when one was safe on dry land; about men battling with the elements when one was snug by the fire. The mystery of death, the adventure of life – she had found the by-pass round both of them; a room with painted vistas, a radiogram softly playing, a final drink, and phht! that was the end of Clare Bentley. The following Feet, if they existed, could never catch up with her, for the simple reason that there would be nothing to catch up with...

The door of her room was flung open without ceremony; Stephen entered, slammed the door shut, set his back against it, and snarled:

"You stupid, bloody fool! Don't say I didn't warn you."

Anger boiled up in her.

"Now look here, Stephen, I've had about enough of your rudeness. After last night I'm not in the mood to listen to diatribes. And for the rest of my time at Fremley, I'd be obliged if you'd leave me alone. I don't want your company – "

"There rest of your time here, my good girl, consists of this evening and tonight. You're off first thing tomorrow morning."

Her anger died as though quenched by cold water.

"I don't know what you mean by that, Stephen. I may have talked an awful lot of nonsense earlier, but I've decided to stay. I'm going to tell Mr Reddington so – "

He interrupted by striding across to her, took her roughly by the shoulders, and standing over her, said in a voice that shook with an emotion the nature of which was not entirely clear to her:

"For a supposedly intelligent woman, you're about the most naïve creature I've ever met. You gave yourself away to the Lord High in the early hours of this morning for a start. 'It wasn't like that at all,' you said, when he was raging about Peter's coming here on false pretences. Oh, the Lord High didn't seem to pay any attention; but he has the most uncanny knack of registering any unguarded remark. It was obvious that you and Peter were buddies."

"You're a fine one to talk," snapped Clare. "What if we were buddies, as you call it, which in point of fact we weren't. Before ever Peter came here you were telling me about how happy they we in the Hebrides; and then there was all that about the possibility of life after death you were prattling abut here in this very room."

"*I* pick my company when I'm going to prattle."

"But what *is* all this?" she cried, thumping her fist on the cushion. "You're simply trying to frighten me for some reason or other. Peter tried to hang himself; well, that may be some sort of a misdemeanour, but it can't be a crime. And anyway they can't possibly make me a party to it and even if they did, they can't touch me, not while I'm here at Fremley."

"Exactly! While you're here, you're as good as dead, officially written off the list of citizens. So they tempt you to come out voluntarily into the world again, and you fall for it, hook, line, and sinker."

She threw her hand across her mouth.

"The doctor – "

"Happens also to be an official from the Ministry of Security. Happens to have had a briefcase with him, which happens to have contained, concealed under some papers, a miniature tape recorder. 'I would like to leave Fremley,' says you. So the dead Clare becomes the live Clare again; and the live Clare can be called as a witness for the prosecution."

She rose unsteadily. An invisible trap seemed to be closing in on her. Stephen took her by the shoulders again, slightly shaking her, but without his former exasperation. He said deeply:

"You've got to face it, girl. They suspect that Peter contrived to slip over from the Hebrides. That's a crime. They suspect further that he's tried to convert others to Christianity, and that's high treason."

Chapter Two

(i)

The State was efficient; there was no denying that. As it had provided for all Clare's needs when she was one of its Artists, and again when she was a "martyr" in a Home of Rest, so now it took complete charge of her in her new guise, the star witness for the prosecution.

She was whisked away from Fremley in a police helicopter, and in a few minutes was deposited at the air terminal built on the site of Buckingham Palace; thence to a flatlet assigned her in a vast block which had arisen on the foundations of the demolished Tower of London, commanding a view of similar blocks, and the supermarket and bowling alley erected on what had been the moat. At night the neon sign above an artificial fertilizer factory winked at her, informing her over and over again that, "The desert shall blossom as the rose".

From one window she could look down upon the Old Bailey. The figure of Justice had been removed from the roof, and a specimen of modern art substituted, a female figure, or supposedly so, clasping a miniature computer in place of the traditional scales, and of course without the sword. Whether Justice was still blindfolded or not it was impossible to tell, for she had no recognizable face.

A job of some sort had been found for Clare; she was vaguely Art Adviser in one of the State publishing houses. A small pile of ration books awaited her, with a new identity card; and to protect her from the Press and the curiosity-mongers, a flat-mate had been installed, a policewoman disguised as a State Companion. This Sally was as efficient as the computer on the roof of the Old Bailey, a bright young woman who never stopped talking about the glories of the new utopia.

"To think that for hundreds and hundreds of years, dear, there was some stuffy old castle where we live now. Fancy nobody ever thinking of taking it down when there was a housing shortage."

The whole world seemed to Clare curiously inhuman now. Perhaps it was because of the overdose of human nature in the raw which she had encountered at Fremley. Before her going there, she had never found it difficult to accept this technological age and all its blessings; now she found herself noticing lacks, like the curious absence of sunset colours said by some to be due to the banishment of smoke. She had an absurd nostalgia for the warmth of home going up from thousands of chimneys. You had even been able to light a fire just when you felt like it, she remembered. Now everything, even warmth, was regulated by the State. She sat at her window looking over this new London, which hurt the eye with its sameness, a prefabricated City of Man, of Man who had lost his soul.

But mostly she lived in that curious inertia of mind and body which she had experienced after parting from Michael. She was numb, as from a drug. The idea of trying to contact Michael simply did not occur to her, nor was she in the least surprised or hurt when he failed to contact her. He was someone in another life; she was a sort of half-being, in this world and yet not of it. The Clare Bentley whose name the headlines screamed was a stranger; so also was the Peter Diplock whose caricatured features appeared in a hundred cartoons. "All this and Heaven too", sneered the caption beneath a comic picture of Peter entering one of the State brothels, the Houses of Joy, as they were called, with a crucifix dangling from one pocket and from the other protruding a bunch of alcohol coupons, a brothel licence and contraceptives.

Twice a week she had to attend a psychiatric clinic to be groomed for her new role. But now it was no more than going to the dentist to have a tooth stopped; it was always possible that the drill might touch a nerve, but otherwise it was merely uncomfortable and humiliating. Her recurring dream of being chased by something was of surpassing interest to the psychiatrist. He explained that it was, of course, Michael who was chasing her, but such a wish of the Unconscious had been, at Fremley, no longer suitable for Consciousness. It took a fortnight to "break" this dream down, and at the end of that time it had not the remotest resemblance to what Clare had really dreamt at Fremley Manor.

"It is a commonplace, my dear," pontificated the psychiatrist, "that the dream-function is to express an unfulfilled egocentric wish. In sleep what we call the Censor is abrogated, allowing unconscious wishes to take the field; naturally in your case this unconscious wish was for your lover to follow you to the Home of Rest; your Censor compelled him to disguise himself under a symbolic form. I will lend you a work on the Theory of Symbolism; you will find it most helpful."

She smiled dully, and said thank you, thinking: Fixation, phobia, guilt complex, the id, the libido, the super-ego, all these terms he uses so glibly – does he really understand them, or are they just masks for his own ignorance, the terrifying ignorance of the specialist?

When her work was done, she roamed London, escorted by the vigilant Sally. But Clare could shut her ears to Sally's constant eulogizing; she was seeing London with new eyes, remembering Stephen's remark about the general unhappiness on people's faces in this utopia.

The Humanitarian State had given them everything the body and the reason could desire. There was not one ill-nourished, shabby, unemployed, cold, or homeless; all their money worries had been removed, none was over worked. Certainly they lacked individual freedom, but that had entailed insecurity; you could not have it both ways. The State cared for them from the Artificial Insemination clinics in which most of them were hatched, to the atomic pencil which reduced them to nothingness. And it was not as if they lived dull lives; their kindly foster-mother, the State, provided them with free sport, entertainment, spectacles, games.

They could even have religion of a kind, a religion divested, of course, of all mystery. There were various national holidays of obligation, Freedom from War Day, Freedom from Want Day, and the rest, when all must either attend the uplift services or watch them on television; the penalty for not doing so was a fine. Some of the old churches had been turned into shrines of Humanity, notably St Paul's, now called Paul's House, where, in place of the old saints, busts of Marx, Freud, Jung, the pioneers of birth-control, of euthanasia, and other contemporary blessings, looked triumphantly down from their niches, while where the altar had been a vast male figure was enthroned, with the text, "Thou shalt have none other goods but me."

Westminster Cathedral, on the other hand, had been turned into a museum of horrors. It was filled with the worst kind of devotional images, instruments of torture, frescoes depicting sham miracles and the sale of

Indulgences, a confessional-box in which a dummy priest held out a collecting-plate in one hand while fondling a young female penitent with the other. The old gigantic rood had been retained because the emaciated Figure hanging there was the very embodiment of poverty and hunger. Above it, in staring red letters, was painted the text, "Not peace but a sword."

It was all perhaps a little crude, but it certainly appealed to the simple-minded.

(ii)

The case of Peter Diplock threatened a national panic, and a witch hunt was on.

The Ministry of Information did its best, but it could not stop wild rumours from spreading. People saw Christians everywhere, even in the Government; the cranks in the reservations were plotting to invade; there was to be a new Armada; they had even discovered the secret of nuclear power. There was going to be a repetition of the Last World War; there was a gigantic fifth column in Britain. The pathetic little right-wing party, the old Communists, seized joyfully upon the scare and moved a vote of censure. APS appeared twice in one day on television, looking like Queen Victoria at her least amused, and the faint Birmingham accent assured the nation that everything was under control.

But the nation did not want everything to be under control. This was just the kind of drama for which it craved. Now that there was no war, no competition, no juicy divorce court proceedings, no capital punishment, the craving for excitement was scarcely ever satisfied.

No trial for high treason had been held within living memory, and people queued for nearly a week beforehand for the public seats in the Central Criminal Court when, early in the new year, the trial of Peter Diplock commenced.

It was strangely unseasonable weather, humid when it should have been cold, with the sky even more overcast than was usual nowadays. In spite of the air-conditioning, the artificial sunlight outside, and the bright lights within, the court-room seemed both gloomy and oppressive. To the spectators, however, it was as thrilling as a stage-set. The State had a keen sense of what was good to retain in English legal tradition, and what should be abolished, and thus counsel still wore nylon wig and gown, the judges still presided in all the old glory of furred robes and full-bottomed wigs. Their nosegays, however, were plastic, real flowers becoming increasingly scarce; and from above them the inverted sword had been long ago removed.

A very young, unknown barrister had been assigned to the prisoner for his defence; on the other side was the Attorney General, assisted by the Solicitor General and a junior. The shuffle of feet, animated talk, and the buzz of transistors in the public gallery rose to a sustained roar of excitement as limping footsteps could be heard on the stairs leading up to the dock; and a moment later, supported by two warders, the prisoner emerged into the light.

A more pitiable object could scarcely be imagined. He was unshaven, his eyes were red-rimmed and bloodshot as though from continuous weeping, and his hands, ugly with the scars of his self-inflicted wounds, shook violently before he clutched the edge of the dock. His tie, shoelaces and braces had been removed. It had been carefully explained in the Press that so determined had the accused shown himself to end his life by some barbaric method, that he could not be trusted not to attempt it even here.

The preliminaries began. The legal jargon had been somewhat simplified, the Norman-French *Oyez* being abolished, but certain old phrases had been retained as being harmlessly picturesque.

"Attention!" cried the Usher. "My lords, the State's Justices, do strictly charge and command all manner of persons to keep silence, for they will now proceed to the pleas of the State and arraignment of prisoners, and all those who are bound by recognisance to give evidence against any of the prisoners which shall be at the bar, let them come forth and give their evidence."

There was a reluctant switching off of transistors in the public gallery.

The State's Coroner, on whom devolved the duty of holding an inquest into charges of high treason, rapidly read out the long indictment, ending with the formal question as to whether the prisoner pleaded guilty or not guilty. Young Mr Reed, counsel for the defence, rose before Peter could reply.

"Before the prisoner pleads," said he, "I, on his behalf, move to quash the indictment on the ground that no offence known to the law is disclosed in the indictment as framed. It is based upon the Treason Act of 1351; a statute which, we may think, ought to have been abolished. Presumably it was overlooked in the huge task of revising Acts of Parliament, a work which has been going on ever since the Nuclear Disaster. Moreover," he added with an ingratiating smile, "our legislators must have found it difficult to imagine that any citizen of our new utopia would ever be guilty of high treason. However that may be, the prisoner is, in fact, indicted under this ancient statute, which defines treason as 'levying war against the King, or being adherent to the King's enemies, in his realm giving them aid and comfort, or elsewhere'. I respectfully submit that what the prisoner is alleged to have done is not an offence within the meaning of this statute."

The Attorney General glanced sharply at Mr Reed, of whom he had the poorest possible opinion. Who would have thought the fool capable of seizing on this legal quibble? But it was an excellent opportunity for counsel on both sides to air their knowledge and to amuse the Court with extracts from quaint old statutes. Vast and ancient tomes were sent for and consulted; the names of Coke, Hallam, and Blackstone were bandied about. It was discovered that as late as 1914 in indictments for treason the accused had been described as being "moved and seduced by the instigation of the Devil." The Press lapped it up.

"Really," said the Lord Chief Justice reluctantly at last, "I doubt whether we serve any useful purpose in looking too far into these ancient authorities, when we have to deal with the law that binds us now."

They all sighed. It had been good fun, this delving into barbaric ages. The motion to quash the indictment was refused in learned speeches by all three judges, and the prisoner pleaded not guilty in a voice so low that he had to be asked to repeat it. Pressmen and spectators glowered at him; they had wanted a Guy Fawkes figure, malignant and sinister; this wretched little man was going to give them no thrill.

"I must inform you," said the State's Coroner, addressing the prisoner after asking him whether he had been supplied with a copy of the indictment at least ten days previously, "that under the Treason Act of 1695, any person accused of high treason may challenge thirty-five jurors without giving reason, and any number 'for cause', but he or his counsel must do so as the names of such jurors are called out as they come to be sworn."

Peter merely blinked at him; he seemed either drugged or bemused.

The jury, eleven women and one lone male, all of whom looked suitably progressive, were sworn, not on the book, of course, the State having abolished such superstitions, but by raising their right hands, while the Clerk raced through the formula:

"You-shall-well-and-truly-try-and-true-deliverance-make-between-the-State-and-the-prisoner-at-the-bar-whom-you-shall-have-in-charge-and-a-true-verdict-give-according-to-the-evidence."

Interest quickened, as the Attorney General rose to speak.

(iii)

Like most men in high office nowadays, Sir Edward Nibbets was young. He possessed a peculiarly charming voice, and his favourite trick was to lull the jury and witnesses with his dulcet tones and then suddenly to roar at them. It was not a new gimmick, but none had ever used it more effectively.

"May it please your lordship, members of the jury: I appear with my learned friends on behalf of the State to support the charge of high treason against the prisoner at the bar, who has the advantage of being defended by my learned friend, Mr – er – " he pretended to consult his notes " – Mr Reed. It is desirable that you should hear all that is known of the prisoner's antecedents. He is, contrary to what you may imagine from his appearance, an intelligent, well-educated man."

With the aid of his noted, he related the history of Peter. The son of Christian parents, he had done well at school, and at the age of eighteen had gone on to a seminary, being ordained priest just before the Reservations Act;

consequent upon the passing of that Act, he had emigrated voluntarily to the Hebrides, accepting the condition that he must never return to his native land.

"I cannot describe to you his way of life in the Hebrides," continued the Attorney General, "for the State does not interest itself in the activities of these outlaws so long as they keep to their chosen banishment. Nor is it within my power to supply you with details as to how he contrived to return to civilization, despite the watchfulness of the authorities on our coasts. Such details do not really concern you, for the fact that he came, and came of his own free will, is not in dispute. You will learn from the evidence I shall put before you the dire purpose of his coming; it was to seduce from their allegiance to Humanity and to the State as many as possible of our citizens.

"Let me say at once, for your comfort, that, so far as such evidence is available to the State, the majority of those whom he approached, with a view to persuading them to forsake their allegiance, received him with contempt. I say, 'for your comfort'; for," suddenly bellowed Sir Edward, "when you have heard the evidence, the inference will probably be drawn by you that it was intended to use such converts as a trained and instructed nucleus round whom the disaffected section of the population might rally, in order to achieve the overthrowing of this State."

He paused for effect, then went on, reverting to his natural voice:

"The prisoner chose, deliberately, the more emotional or the more uninformed among our citizens, who, he believed, would fall easy victims to his specious promises of what is vulgarly known as 'pie in the sky'. Always there will be, even in the most highly civilized and educated society, a few who are a prey to superstition, or else are by nature discontented. I cannot give you a complete account of the arguments he used; I can only supply such fragments of his appeals as happened to linger in the minds of those whose evidence is available to the State. He tempted his simple dupes with rewards such as, you may think, could have little attraction for any rational man or woman; they were to live for ever and ever in a City with golden streets, somewhere in the clouds, playing harps and engaging in a non-stop community singing; while on the other hand he threatened these poor folk with an alternative eternity of fire and gnawing worms somewhere below this earth."

He waited for the laughter to subside, then pounced again.

"You smile, members of the jury; but do not fall into the mistake of dismissing the accused as unworthy of serious censure. Man, however enlightened, cannot afford to dismiss Christianity as merely absurd, for an absurd thing is bound to die a natural death in course of time. I must remind you that the doctrines preached by the prisoner, divorced from reason though they undoubtedly are, have misled men, yes, even intelligent, cultivated, learned men, for two thousand years. They will do so again unless we are on our guard. It is but recently that Man has thrown off his bondage to the supernatural, has, so to speak, come of age; it would be fatally easy for him to slip back into childishness.

"We cannot tell even yet how many have been seduced by the prisoner; it may well be that some have not dared to come forward. We do not know how many other so-called missionaries in those hot-beds of sedition, the reservations, are contemplating a descent upon us with the same seduction in mind. If, as sometimes happens even in these days when natural ills are all but conquered, a virulent and contagious disease is discovered in our midst, the most stringent precautions are taken against its spreading. No less resolute must we be in stamping out a disease which seeks to plunge men's minds back into medieval darkness. We must not soothe away our fears with the hope that our World Parliament may decide that these cancer-spots must be cut out, that the mercy bomb so much talked of is a necessary act of justice as well as of mental hygiene. Matters brought before the World Parliament occupy much time before they are decided on; and meanwhile we must be vigilant to stamp out this plague where and when we find it."

He turned and looked full at the battered figure in the dock.

"You may think, members of the jury, that the prisoner is sincerely penitent, and is therefore entitled to mercy. It is my duty to inform you that though he professes to be no longer able to believe in the pernicious doctrines in which he was brought up, yet he has steadily refused to disclose the names of those whom he has 'reconciled', as he calls it, to the Christian Church, or the means by which he contrived to cross over from the Hebrides. Is this repentance? Thus there is a grave hiatus in the information which the State is in a position to lay before you; yet there is enough, and more than enough, to prove to you that even to the end, as he thought, of his life, he continued his odious work of corrupting, or seeking to corrupt, the minds of our citizens."

He sat down, and the State called its first witnesses.

These had little of interest to say, and defence counsel's, "I have no questions", became monotonous. Officials appeared who testified that they had examined Peter and supplied him with the necessary passports when he had gone to the Hebrides originally. By way of divorcing public sympathy from the accused, several were then called to testify to his corrupt way of life since his apostasy, his buying of drug, alcohol, and contraceptive coupons on the black market, and his frequenting of the Houses of Joy.

Here, said the prosecution in effect, is your typical Christian. But the papers had supplied such juicy details for months past, and nothing new emerged. It was when succeeding witnesses began to speak of Peter's missionizing, that the public sat up and took notice.

"I teach Family Planning in a primary school," said a young woman in canary-coloured ski-pants and a "lion-mane" hair style. "One of my kids who's gone on to secondary, came to me in a flap and said she'd met a type in a coffee-bar who'd told her that the abortion she was due to have was murder."

There were gasps of incredulous horror from the gallery.

"She was always a mixed-up kid," continued the school teacher, "so of course I thought she was trying to pull a fast one. Still, just for a giggle, I thought I'd meet this type, so I went to the coffee-bar and this kid pointed him out."

"Do you see the type – the man – in Court?"

"Yeah, that's him in the dock. Well, he seemed to me a nut-case. I mean to say, when I tackled him, he up and said to my face that abortion, even though it was authorized by the State, was what he called 'the murder of the unborn'."

"I have no questions," almost groaned Mr Reed.

A timid woman of uncertain age came next.

"My mother," she said, "was a Roman Catholic; at least, of course I mean she was before Christianity was outlawed. She takes in lodgers, or rather she did before she fell ill; she's in a Rehabilitation Centre now, and that's why she can't come to Court. Well, one day last summer, in August I think it was, she let a room to a man."

"Do you see that man here?" enquired the Solicitor General.

"Yes, sir, I see him there in the dock. Well, my mother came to me one evening when I got home from work, and told me that this man was a priest and that he was going to say Mass in her room, and she asked me to fetch some bread. I said I had heard they used only special wafers – "

"I object," Mr Reed interrupted smartly. "The witness is reporting hearsay."

The objection was sustained, and the witness, more frightened than ever, gabbled:

"My mother said that the missionaries had special privileges; they could use any kind of bread, say Mass without candles, and with any sort of vessels that could be destroyed, like glass or china, but not plastic, and they had a portable altar of wood, and they didn't have to use vestments, except a sort of thread representing the stole, of all the liturgical colours woven together, and though I wouldn't go to Mass," concluded the witness virtuously, "I did see the stole, for my mother showed it to me."

Exhibit 3 was handed to her, and was identified as the stole in question.

The next witness, a bearded young man, was more interesting. In common with most of the population nowadays, he was employed in one of the Ministries, and lived in a State Hostel. The deliciously horrified spectators heard him swear that he had actually been present when the accused had said Mass secretly in the Hostel in the early hours of the morning. The defence made a gallant effort to shake his testimony.

"How do you know he was saying Mass?"

"He had this stole on, and he was talking Latin."

"Do you understand Latin?"

"No," said the young man grumpily.

"Was the room dark during this – er – ceremony?"

"It was pretty dark."

"Then how can you positively identify the man who presided?"

There was no reply, but the Attorney General was not worried. He had half a dozen other witnesses up his sleeve.

To some the prisoner had defended Christianity; one had actually been to confession to him.

"Why did you go?" demanded Sir Edward.

"Oh, just for kicks," the witness hastened to answer. "And I heard him preach a sort of sermon, all about Christ's weeping over Jerusalem, or some such place, and foretelling its destruction. What he meant was, this bloke in the dock, I mean, that Brotherhood would be destroyed in the same way – "

Mr Reed leapt up as though pricked by a pin, but before he had time to object, the Lord Chief Justice said emphatically:

"The witness cannot possibly know what the accused meant by this parable. The jury will disregard it."

No one was going to be able to say that the prisoner had not had a scrupulously fair trial.

When the Court adjourned till next morning, there was a fight to form a queue outside for seats in the gallery. The public appetite had been nicely whetted for the feast to come, the inside story of a Home of Rest, and actually two witnesses who had gone there to self-eliminate.

Chapter Three

The first witness called by the State next morning was the psychologist attached to the Detention Centre where Peter had been since his arrest. He was asked a simple question: was the prisoner of unsound mind? It took him half an hour to answer, bemusing the Court with his technical terms, but it finally emerged that Peter, though definitely abnormal, was quite as definitely sane.

There followed him the Euthanasia Referee who had presided over the Board of Investigation before whom Peter had appeared after his application to go to a Home of Rest. Defence counsel made the most of the opportunity to side-track the issue; it must be a matter of grave public concern, said Mr Reed, that a Board who were responsible for the lives of men and women, who had to distinguish between genuine martyrs and impostors, had so far failed in the case of the accused, that but for unexpected circumstances his name would have been read out from the honoured roll on Remembrance Day. There were some very hot exchanges, and the Euthanasia Referee grew so abusive that the Bench was obliged to intervene.

The silence was intense when Frederick Reddington was called, and everyone craned to get a better look at him. His wholesomeness, his pinkness, his neat bow tie and well-

173

pressed dark suit, his cosy, paternal manner, all were infinitely reassuring to those among the public who had lost relatives by self-elimination. It was greatly to Mr Reddington's credit that he gave this impression today, for actually he was in dread lest he be blamed for not discovering that Peter had come from the Hebrides.

"Mr Reddington," said the Attorney General suavely, when the Custodian of Fremley had identified the prisoner, "did you have any serious conversation with the accused between the time of his coming to Fremley and its attempt to – er – make an end of his life in an improper manner?"

"I did not," replied Mr Reddington. "It is not my business to force confidences; my task is to comfort and assist our martyrs in their preparation for their great self-sacrifice. If they wish to seek my advice or my encouragement, I am at their service at any hour; otherwise, I respect their privacy. The prisoner was extremely reserved, at least with me. There was only one incident which somewhat disturbed me."

"Will you please describe it?"

"It was on the evening of his arrival. It happened to be Remembrance Day, which of course at our Homes of Rest is celebrated with the greatest possible solemnity. After laying a wreath on our local Memorial, and when our guests had seen our beloved Prime Minister addressing the nation on television, I gave them a little homely talk which I hoped would both comfort and inspire them. I must confess that I was so carried away by the occasion, that I did not notice when one of our guests, the prisoner, hurriedly left the room. It was only afterwards that my assistant called me to help deal with the prisoner, who had become extremely excited."

Mr Reddington paused, swallowed, and continued, with a heightened pink:

"I knew, of course, or I should say now that I thought I knew, all the details of the prisoner's case. Naturally I have to rely entirely on the information I receive from the Euthanasia Referee, who, I understand, was himself deceived by the prisoner. But I knew that he, I mean the accused, had been at one time a Popish priest, had lost faith in his foolish, I may say wicked, beliefs, but being unable to adjust himself to our beautiful sane modern world, had received permission to self-eliminate. His antecedents being such, I thought it excusable that my little talk, combined with the events of the day, should have made him hysterical. He said, for instance, that the word euthanasia did not mean 'easy and gentle death', but 'dying well': this I put down to his ignorance; and when he used such terms as 'suicide' and 'self-murder', I took the poor fellow to be raving. I endeavoured to be patient even when he – er – actually offered me some physical violence."

This produced a great sensation. The pressmen's ball-points galloped, several thrusting their way out of Court to rush to the telephone, while the public in the gallery struggled for a fresh view of this extraordinary prisoner who had actually tried to hit the Custodian of the best run Home of Rest in Britain.

"With the aid of a sedative," Mr Reddington went on, "I succeeded in calming him down, and next morning he appeared to have regained control of himself. I was, I must confess, a little disappointed when he failed to offer me an apology, but I have learned to be tolerant and understanding with such of our dear martyrs who do not immediately find the atmosphere at Fremley soothing, and I hoped that during the ensuing fortnight the prisoner would feel the benefit of our treatment, and discover that perfect peace which the world could not give him."

Mr Reddington made a reverent pause, somewhat spoilt by the asperity which he could not keep from his voice as he concluded:

"The very next night, he attempted that disgusting act which has since become common knowledge, and which caused our genuine martyrs and their loved ones acute pain and distress."

He was led tactfully through the finding of Peter, identified the crucifix and rosary found on the accused when he was cut down insensible, and now exhibited by the State, and was turned over to the defence. Mr Reed foolishly decided to cross-examine.

"Mr Reddington, during the time the accused was in your care, did he, on any occasion, endeavour to convert you to Christianity?"

"My dear sir!"

"Kindly answer the question."

"He did not," boomed Mr Reddington emphatically, his pink turning to an angry red. "Even he must have known better than that."

"Nor, to your knowledge, did he attempt this with any of your – er – guests?"

"Had he done so, I assure you that I should have telephoned immediately to the Ministry of Self-Elimination."

"Yet I understand the prosecution contends that attempts were made by the prisoner, not altogether unsuccessfully, to proselytize at Fremley. You deny this?"

"I deny my knowledge of it at the time," snapped Mr Reddington. "I do not spy upon my guests, sir; I do not eavesdrop upon them, or force their confidences... "

The Court was treated to a further description of Fremley, its peace, privacy, and freedom, before Mr Reddington could be induced to stand down and give place to his wife.

Mrs Reddington, looking motherly in tweeds and an unfashionably shaped hat, had little to add to the testimony of her spouse. She was obliged to make use of a clean handkerchief, soaked in eau de Cologne, during her description of the finding of Peter, and gently amused the Court by her naïve lamenting over her ruined carpet. On the whole the public decided that the Reddingtons were the kind of folk with whom they could entrust their last days if ever they felt like self-elimination; and the Court adjourned for lunch.

(ii)

The witness called immediately after the lunch recess did not promise to be very interesting. She was definitely an aunt-figure, dim, drab, domesticated; grey hair was twisted into a tight bun under her hat which was actually fastened by a large pin; one felt sure that she wore woollen combinations. She carried a shabby bag, from which protruded a pair of knitting-needles; and she wore cheap cotton gloves. One of the papers reported afterwards that there was a darn on the back of her gloves, but that was a little too much to credit. Nobody darned, or repaired, anything nowadays; when things wore out they were simply thrown away.

But as soon as this Mrs Jane Smith entered the box, she created a sensation. She lifted one of her gloved hands and waved it to the sorry creature in the dock, and she smiled at him. It was a smile that lit her commonplace features, and made her for a moment almost beautiful.

"Mr Attorney," said the Lord Chief Justice, "I understand that this witness was an inmate of the Home of Rest during the time the prisoner resided there. How comes it, therefore, that she is considered by the State to be an eligible witness?"

"If it please your lordship," replied the dulcet voice, "both this witness, and another I shall call presently, have applied for a cancellation of their certificate authorizing them to self-eliminate."

"I understand," murmured the Lord Chief Justice; but he was not really sure that he did.

Sir Edward Nibbets himself rose to examine.

"Mrs Smith," he purred, "will you tell the Court, in your own words, what conversation you had at Fremley Manor with the prisoner at the bar?"

She laid her hands lightly on the edge of the box, and began at once. Of all the witnesses so far, she was the only one who appeared absolutely natural and self-confident.

"I found Mr Peter ever so sympathetic. I got talking about my children, and especially about Tom (that's my youngest boy), who's ever so clever, and you know, most people find it boring when you go on and on about your children, and of course it is. Like showing lots of family snapshots. But he didn't – find it boring, I mean. And then afterwards, somebody said to me, or I heard it somehow, that he'd been a Popish priest."

She paused, frowning a little as though at a private memory.

"Well, it gave me quite a turn. I mean, my lord, if you understand me," she said, personally addressing the Lord Chief Justice, whom she described afterwards as having ever such a kind face, "I was brought up a strict Protestant. And I taxed him with it when we was alone in the Sun Lounge that afternoon. It's not right, I said, all this praying to this saint and that; we don't need no saints, I said, I mean we didn't when we were Christians, because there oughtn't to be anyone between ourselves and the Lord. Well, I'll try and remember what Mr Peter answered, in his own words. He said, 'When I was a boy, I always had a terror of the sea, and it was arranged that I should go for a holiday in Ireland. The only thing I held on to during the horror of that crossing was the knowledge that my elder brother, who had always been a hero to me, had gone over before me. I knew he was thinking about me all the time, and praying for me. The saints are like that,' he said; 'they have crossed' – now what was it? oh yes! – 'the ocean of our mortality before us'."

Mrs Smith smiled round the Court.

"Well, I thought that was ever such a nice idea, I really did. But I hadn't done with him yet. That's all very well, I said, but what about your worship of the Virgin Mary? It's not right, I said; why, you've only got to read the Bible and you'll see how Jesus thought about *her*. Ever so snappy, He was, when she spoke, and called her 'Woman'. He smiled a bit at that (this Mr Peter, I mean), and asked did I know that in Hebrew it was like calling someone 'Lady' in English?"

She nodded at the Lord Chief Justice, inviting him to partake in her surprise.

"Yes. 'Well,' I said, 'I don't know about that, but if you read the Gospels, where is she? You don't hardly hear of her at all,' I said, 'so she can't be all that important.' 'Mrs Smith,' he said, with that rather sad smile of his, 'you talked to me for a full hour this morning about your son Tom. There wasn't a word about yourself.' 'Why no,' I said, 'because I'm only his mother, and Tom's – well, Tom's ever so clever. Why should I want to talk about myself when there's Tom?' 'Yes,' he said, 'that's really the point, isn't it? A true mother always likes to keep in the background. And isn't that what you'd expect,' he said, 'of the Mother of God? There was only one thing she did say about herself,' he said, 'and that was the simple statement that henceforth all generations would call her blessed. Not that she'd want them to, but that they'd do it naturally out of love for her Son.' "

"I confess I do not comprehend the purport of this evidence," remarked Mr Justice Fraser suddenly.

"My lord, with your lordship's permission," soothed the Attorney General, "I intend to prove that the prisoner did, in fact, seek to convert others to Christianity even when he himself was contemplating self-elimination. Now, Mrs Smith, you were telling us what the prisoner said to you."

"Yes, well," continued Mrs Smith, only slightly put out of her stride, "I said to Mr Peter, 'It still doesn't seem right to me to pray to the Virgin Mary.' 'If someone wanted to ask a favour of your son Tom,' he said, 'don't you think it would be natural for them to ask you to put in a good word for them with him? That's all we do when we pray to Our Lady.' "

Suddenly the patient face crumpled, and the tears ran down. She fished in her bag for a clean handkerchief, and wiped them away.

"I'm ever so sorry, my lord. It's just that no one would ever ask me to put in a good word with any of my boys now. They don't need me no more, not for anything. I said something about that to Mr Peter and he said did I remember that the Mother of Jesus stood at the foot of the Cross? 'You've got to wait and be patient, Mrs Smith,' he said; 'one day Tom may need you when he's in sore trouble, just to stand beside him when there's no one else.' Well, it was that, my lord, that made me ask to come out of the Home of Rest; you see, it would be awful for Tom to need me, and me not to be there, through my own fault."

"Mr Attorney," said the Lord Chief Justice, "I am reluctant to intervene, but unless the defence wishes to cross-examine, I do not think this witness should be subjected to further questioning."

"I have no questions," Mr Reed said automatically.

"I hope," continued his lordship, "that this witness has been suitably provided for. She seems a very good sort of woman."

"I understand, my lord, that she has been appointed house-mother in a Home for Backward Boys. It is obvious that she has a mother-fixation."

"But I *am* a mother," said Mrs Smith reasonably, as she stepped down from the box.

Really, thought the Attorney General, what an incurable old sentimentalist is the LCJ! It was high time he retired. This new Age Elimination Bill which was proposed for all over sixty...too old, decided Sir Edward, thinking of his own father, of that tendency to repeat himself, that increasing deafness, that maddening "What say?" Fifty would be far more humane, thought the Attorney General, who was a comfortable thirty-four.

(iii)

As a complete contrast to the pathetic Mrs Smith, there came a man with a saturnine face and an air of vague insolence, who gave his name as Stephen Coles. He had been, it appeared, assistant to Mr Reddington at Fremley Manor, a post of which he had now been relieved. He was asked about his previous work.

"Before I went to Fremley, I was Sports Instructor at a Reformation Centre. I found that the prisoners – I beg your pardon – the patients were not interested in games; at least not the sort it was my job to teach them."

"And your present occupation?"

"Oh, I've been demoted. I'm now Amusements Officer at an Animals' Holiday Camp. They still seem to appreciate games."

"The witness will confine himself to answering questions," intervened the Lord Chief Justice sharply.

"As assistant to Mr Reddington, you had a good deal to do with the guests at Fremley Manor?"

"It was my job to gauge the amount of dope needed to keep 'em quiet and – "

"Mr Coles, you have already been rebuked by his lordship. Will you kindly give me a plain yes or no?"

"Yes, I had."

"Cast your mind back to the evening of November 1st. The prisoner made some disturbance, we have been told, in the Television Room that evening. You were present?"

"Yes. He got up during Mr Reddington's – homily, and by his looks I thought he was ill. I helped him to his room, and attempted to pacify him."

"He was angry and abusive?"

"He was certainly angry; he was not abusive with me."

"About what was he angry?"

Stephen hesitated. Then he said in clipped tones:

"He complained of blasphemy. He was somewhat incoherent, but I understood him to mean Mr Reddington's twisting certain passages from Scripture and applying them to self-eliminators. I did what I could for him, but in the end I felt obliged to fetch Mr Reddington."

"For what purpose?"

"To give him an extra strong dose of mercy drug. I wasn't allowed to – "

"Quite so. And the prisoner took it willingly, I have no doubt. Now – "

"I beg your pardon. I feel bound to state that he did not take it willingly. Considerable compulsion had to be used."

The Attorney General rustled his notes and changed the subject.

"Did you have any further conversation with the prisoner?"

"Only one. I happened to remark on the general restlessness of people nowadays; this was apropos of the increasing use of tranquillizers and pep pills. He smiled, and murmured, 'Thou hast made us for Thyself, and our hearts are restless until they find their rest in Thee.' I was struck by the quotation and asked him where it came from. He said it was St Augustine."

"You would call yourself an intelligent man, Mr Coles?" enquired Sir Edward, curling his lip.

"I wouldn't say I was exactly dim-witted."

"And yet you were 'struck' by this absurd quotation, this misleading and entirely meaningless – nay, I will go further, this mischievous quotation, from a Christian saint?"

"Yes," said Stephen deliberately, "I was."

Counsel for the defence, clutching at the flimsiest straw, asked:

"Mr Coles, did the prisoner make any serious attempt to convert you to the Christian religion?"

"He did not."

"Did anything he said, or did, while in your company cast doubts in your mind concerning our modern ideals?"

"Nothing that he said. Something that he did increased the doubts I already had concerning Humanity worship. I refer to his, to me, touching penitence at the end. He wanted to make some sort of sacrifice, however feeble, to atone for what he considered his betrayal of his God. It does seem to me that sacrifice is an essential instinct – "

"Mr Reed," reproved a voice from the Bench, "I feel bound to intervene. The witness is being led to incriminate himself."

Mr Reed, forcing a ghastly smile, sat down abruptly.

"Miss Clare Bentley," said the Attorney General.

This was the witness for whom the public had been waiting. A youngish woman, easy on the eye; at one time a State Artist; a candidate for self-elimination because of a

183

hopeless love; her lover with a wife in a Mental Home. And now a sort of female Lazarus, risen almost from the dead. Oh yes, she was a star turn, was Miss Clare Bentley. For months she had been front page news; "Clare cancels her own death-warrant", ran a banner headline, and a popular cartoon had portrayed her as the Virgin, with Mr Reddington as St John, in a new version of "The Taking down from the Cross". A pity she hadn't her little dog with her; Dragon, too, had been excellent copy.

She was carefully made up, and perhaps it was the strip lighting that made her look pale. (The weather was even more unseasonable than yesterday, with a sky like dull copper, and the temperature soaring towards seventy degrees.) She shot one glance at the dock while she was being sworn; some said afterwards that it was a glance of strange appeal as though she were willing the poor wretch there to stand up for himself. Then she lowered her eyes and kept them downcast.

The Attorney General was tact personified. He asked the minimum of questions regarding her past history (to the intense disappointment of the spectators); his voice was as soothing as that of a running brook as he questioned her about her conversations with the man called Peter.

"You have just told us, Miss Bentley, that when the prisoner made his sudden appearance in the park during your walk there, you were frightened. Why was that?"

"It was because of a – a particularly vivid dream I had had, that someone was chasing me."

This was not what the Attorney General was after, and he frowned. Unlike the psychiatrists, he was not in the least interested in dreams.

"I suggest that you were frightened because the prisoner had been threatening you with eternal punishment, with (I beg your lordships' pardon) Hell, in fact."

"No, the prisoner had said nothing to me about that."

"What was your conversation with him on this second occasion?"

She did not immediately reply. She raised her head and looked directly at the prisoner, and again there was that strange, urgent appeal in her eyes. I've got to say it, she thought desperately; oh do understand and back me up. Don't be the sort of Peter-Judas you were at Fremley; please be just Peter now, hot-headed, cowardly, infirm of purpose, human...

"He told me he had come from the Hebrides."

A deep-drawn sigh, a spontaneous "A-ah!" ran through the crowded court-room. God damn and blast her, prayed defence counsel, forgetting himself; there goes whatever I had of a case.

"You are quite sure he made that admission, Miss Bentley?" pressed the Attorney General. "Remember that you are on oath."

"I am quite sure," she replied, her head downbent again.

"What further conversation had you?"

"I said I supposed that no one could be content to stay in the reservations because of the conditions there, but he said that I misunderstood him. The Founder of Christianity had commanded His followers to go out and teach all nations, and from that day to this there had always been missionaries."

"And he admitted to you that he was one of these – er – missionaries?"

"Not in so many words. But that is what I understood him to mean. He certainly implied it."

Sir Edward permitted himself a smile of satisfaction. He paused to allow what she had said to sink in, and then suddenly changed to his bullying tone.

"When the prisoner made these admissions to you, why did you not inform Mr Reddington?"

"They were made to me in confidence."

"You were aware, of course, that the prisoner, in leaving the reservations for the purpose of spreading his horrible doctrines, had committed a grave crime, and that it was your duty to inform the authorities?"

"I had no longer any duties, in that sense. I was officially dead – and so was the prisoner."

"I ask you to look at Exhibit 6," said the Attorney General, handing her a bold-stained New Testament. "May I ask why you did not hand this book over immediately you found it in the prisoner's room?"

"I wanted to have a look at it. I wanted to find out what the Christians had – well, to say for themselves."

"I suggest to you that you would not have wished to read this book unless the prisoner had already half converted you to Christianity by his talk."

"That isn't true. I was simply – curious."

"Miss Bentley, did anything that the prisoner said to you, or anything you read in this book, made you wonder whether there was truth in the Christian religion?"

"What I read made me wish it *could* be true."

"Thank you, Miss Bentley," said Sir Edward, with a significant glance at the jury. "That is all."

Defence did not cross-examine. Poor Mr Reed had all he could do to make his opening speech.

(iv)

Though he had been warned that the State was determined to make this a test case, and that a plea of insanity would not be entertained, Mr Reed, with the defiance of the desperate, was basing his defence on the grounds that the accused could not be held responsible for his actions. To back this up, he had got hold of one solitary witness, a psychologist who had broken away from the orthodox school, and had invented a psychotherapeutic system of his own.

Mr Reed began by admitting that it had been proved that the prisoner had come over from the Hebrides, and from the testimony of certain witnesses it had transpired that his object in coming over was to missionize. But, went on Mr Reed, it had also been proved that the prisoner, in the glorious atmosphere of Humanity and Brotherhood, had seen the error of his ways, and, too weak to accept this creed and take his place in the community, had applied, quite genuinely, for permission to self-eliminate. His attempt to hang himself was certainly a misdemeanour, but it was irrelevant to the charge of treason, and the manner of the attempt was such as surely proved that the balance of the man's mind was gravely disturbed. The jury would hear a witness testify that this, in fact, was so.

Surely it would be in accordance with the merciful tenets of Humanity, continued Mr Reed, to treat this poor creature as one who was mentally ill, and give him a second chance to get into touch with contemporary thought with the help of experts. He had, though unwittingly, brought home once more to all men the malice of Christians on the one hand, and the total inadequacy (to use no stronger term) of their beliefs on the other, and thus had been of service to the weak who might be tempted to slide back into those superstitions In five months' time of living among the enlightened, he had turned in revolt against the religion in which he had been bred, and of which he was a minister.

"I appreciate how difficult it is that you should be put into a position to understand what goes on in the mind of a Christian. But, members of the jury, you have to try a man for his intentions, for the intention of the accused is the whole substance of treason. Therefore, when you come to consider what is alleged against the prisoner here, you will always have to weigh it, so far as is humanly possible for you to do so, for the purpose of ascertaining with regard to each overt act, what did Peter Diplock do that for? What was his motive? All the witnesses have agreed that he did not ask them to disturb the peace of the land; he was concerned, it seems, solely with what my learned friend, the Attorney General, has so wittily called 'pie in the sky'. Several have testified that the prisoner counselled them to obey the civil powers, in accordance with the command of the itinerant preacher who founded Christianity, and who, according to the Gospels, ordered His followers to render unto Caesar the things which were Caesar's."

He caught Sir Edward's sardonic eye upon him, and floundered.

"Whether, in fact, Christians in general follow this teaching is another question; but we are here, not to try Christians in general, but one man who has since repudiated that creed."

He ended with a necessarily feeble attempt to draw a red herring across the trail.

"What is, or is not, high treason, depends upon the political complexion of the times. Hence many were executed for this crime by Oliver Cromwell for their loyalty to the King; whereas after Charles II was restored, others were executed for their loyalty to Oliver Cromwell. Similarly, after the invasion of King William III... " And so on. He could quote history every bit as well as the Attorney General.

He spun it out, poor man, for another quarter of an hour, though conscious that the jury had never heard of most of the historical personages he was citing, and that the spectators were restless. Then he called his witness.

This Professor Kindhorn had invented new names for the components of the mind, so that nobody really knew what he was talking about. It did finally emerge, however, that in his considered opinion the prisoner was suffering from a definite neurosis, the chief symptom of which was exhibitionism, and that he could not be held responsible for his actions. The State having asked and received permission to recall their own psychologist, a furious quarrel developed between the two experts, to the delight of the public in the gallery. Stephen also was recalled, as the person who had had most to do with Peter at Fremley, and questioned more closely about the prisoner's behaviour there with a view to proving that he was perfectly sane. This was a mistake on the part of the prosecution.

"My lord," said Stephen, blandly addressing the Bench, "I am in a real difficulty about answering these questions. I was employed in a Home of Rest; all our guests at Fremley had been given permission to eliminate themselves by a Board composed of psychologists. Our entire national life nowadays is run, surely, on the assumption that psychology is infallible. Who am I to disagree with the experts, or to choose between them?"

Having thus confused the issue, and sown in the public mind the horrible suspicion that certain self-eliminated loved ones ought not to have been given permission to take their own lives, Stephen, now thoroughly disliked by both sides, was told to stand down, and the Court was adjourned.

Chapter Four

"Members of the jury, I shall not detain you long," promised Mr Reed next morning.

He was haggard from a sleepless night; jokes about the way he was handling the case had finished his career, and he knew it. Several times during the past night he had wondered whether it would not be best of him to apply for self-elimination.

"The crucial question you have to determine when you retire to consider your verdict, is, did the prisoner commit high treason by adhering to, or giving comfort and aid to, the State's enemies? We are dealing with a statute passed seven hundred years ago, and the meaning of the words, 'aid and comfort', is, I suggest to you, something very different today from what it was then. Aiding and comforting – "

"I am most loath to intervene," said the Lord Chief Justice, and he meant it, for he was sorry for the poor man, "but I must remind you, Mr Reed, that the words of the stature are, of course, to be interpreted according to law, and therefore are not for the jury, but for us. Any act which weakens, or tends to weaken, the power of the State, is giving aid and comfort to its enemies. That is the direction of law which in intend to give."

"I am much obliged to; your lordship," murmured Mr Reed, twisting his tobacco-stained fingers together. He would have given the soul in which he did not believe for a cigarette at this moment, and it tortured him to see the public smoking in the gallery. "Members of the jury, the State has to satisfy you, not by surmise, but by evidence and facts proved to your satisfaction, that when the prisoner came over from the Hebrides, he was acting from a motive of desiring to weaken the power of this State. If you are satisfied that his motive in coming over was not an intention to weaken the State, then it is open to you to return a verdict of not guilty. Each one of you must be satisfied that the State have proved their case, and proved it up to the hilt."

He went back over the evidence, picking pathetic little holes here and there, doing his best, poor wretch, to make mountains out of molehills and bricks without straw.

"Finally I feel obliged to make an appeal to your mercy. The prisoner's conduct at Fremley Manor when, having deliberately mutilated his hands and feet, he attempted to hang himself, proves him to be mentally unstable, and therefore not completely responsible for his actions, even if he is sane. And you must remember that as regards his sanity, the experts have disagreed. Surely you, who have the good fortune to be members of a community to whom mental illness is no more blameworthy than the common cold, would wish to see this unfortunate man placed in a psychopathic home rather than in a Reformation Centre."

He sketched a bow to the Bench and sat down, his shaking fingers fishing in his pockets for pockets for a packet of pep pills.

"I must congratulate my learned friend," said the Attorney General cruelly, "on the eloquence with which he has presented the case for the defence, in a speech in which you may, I think, find some indication that even he was conscious of the weakness of the case he was recommending to your convictions. By his emotional appeal to you at the end, my learned friend admitted that weakness."

Sir Edward then spent a solid hour in going through the evidence for the prosecution.

"I do not pretend," he went on, "to recall the admirable language in which my lord, the Lord Chief Justice, gave to my learned friend the direction he proposed to give you on the question of law. But I do remember my lord said this, that he should direct you that anything was aiding and comforting the State's enemies which weakens, or tends to weaken, the power of this State. I ask you to apply that test to what you know from the evidence. The pillars of this State are Humanity and Reason; those are the twin foundations on which it rests. Christianity is founded upon superstition and unreason; it is pledged to dethrone Man and set in his place an idol. It would hurl us back into the dark ages before Man discovered that he was autonomous. It would make us slaves to the supernatural. It glorifies those very things which we detest; patriotism, a prime cause of war, celibacy, which is a denial of the rights of the body, fear of an hereafter which we have proved does not exist, poverty and pain which we have abolished. Man is Lord of the World; he has tamed Nature – "

Like a challenge, pat on his words, there sounded a low growl of thunder, and as he was about to continue, first a faint flicker of lightning made him blink, and then, without warning, every light in the court-room went out.

Sir Edward was so angry that he suddenly found himself longing for a personal God. Nothing less could satisfy his spleen. One could not be angry with the vague thing called Nature; he felt that he had been mocked. The more so when candles, actually candles, had to be lit until the electricians could locate the fuse.

"When we are considering these contingencies," he resumed, with a decided edge to his charming voice (he had to peer at his notes in this antiquated light, and found that he had lost his place), "when we are attempting to understand motives and appraise expectations, we must not confine ourselves to what we know now, that, in fact, the prisoner's attempts to seduce our citizens very largely failed. Suppose they had succeeded? Suppose he had been able to start an epidemic of this death-dealing plague? Do you think it would not have weakened the power of this State?"

He shuffled his notes and came across a chit from the Ministry of Self-Elimination. The public image of this had been damaged during the course of the trial, and the Attorney General would kindly restate the case for it.

"Moreover, members of the jury, you must not forget that the prisoner has been able to seduce, or at least partially to seduce, certain individuals, not all of them of low intelligence. Miss Bentley, once a favourite State Artist, has admitted in evidence that she would *like* to believe in Christianity. And there is the worthy woman, Mrs Smith; the mischievous talk of the prisoner so disturbed what should have been the tranquil termination of the lives of both these witnesses, so discouraged them from their supreme sacrifice, that they have been persuaded to return to a world where they are no longer needed, cannot be useful, and therefore will not find peace.

"Consider, members of the jury, the cruelty of these Christians on the one hand, and the mercy of Humanity upon the other. I must recall to your minds the long and bitter struggle our early Euthanatists had to wage before an easy and gentle death was made legal for those who expressed a wish to be released from acute bodily suffering.

It was a step in the right direction, but ah, what a small one! In the bad old days it was not bodily but mental anguish which caused men and women to take the law into their own hands and 'commit suicide'. Alas, man's inhumanity to man, members of the jury!" cried Sir Edward, his voice breaking with emotion. "But now, thank Brotherhood, we have a Service of Mercy such as the pioneers of Euthanasia would wonder at, for it goes far beyond their dreams; we have our Homes of Rest, where our dear martyrs may find that peace which, as Mr Reddington so touchingly put it, the world cannot give them. And yet here you have these Christians," he suddenly roared, "the followers of one who constantly preached mercy and relieved suffering wherever he found it, daring to insist that their God sent suffering into the world, daring to call self-elimination self-murder!"

The Attorney General blinked again, as the lights came on as abruptly as they had failed.

"Even at the end, members of the jury, you see the prisoner at his tricks, trying to disturb the serenity of our martyrs, trying to convert them, though he himself had what he called apostatized; once a Christian, always a Christian. My learned friend on the other side has suggested to you that the prisoner's loathsome attempt to take his own life at Fremley proves him to be mentally ill. You may think on the other hand that it proves him fettered to his superstitions, for he endeavoured to kill himself in somewhat the same manner in which the Founder of Christianity died. One witness, in speaking of this, mentioned the word 'sacrifice' – surely the language of savages. Enlightened Man does not need to offer sacrifices to appease the non-existent gods. But a Christian can never be enlightened; if we look into history, we see how his superstitions are deeply embedded... "

Here Sir Edward gave a little lecture, ranging through the centuries in a very erudite manner, not neglecting to bring in such purple passages as the Spanish Inquisition, the Gunpowder Plot, Bloody Mary, and the Armada.

"Thus history teaches us that on numerous occasions these Christians have secretly invaded this country with fair words on their lips but with daggers up their sleeves. Man has outlawed war; God, it seems, has not. With him it will be always, 'Not peace but a sword' …

"You may marvel, members of the jury, at the base ingratitude of these Christians. They have been given land where they are free to practise their barbarous rites in peace; they are neither spied upon nor in any way molested; in they enjoy none of the amenities of civilized life, that is because they have rejected the supremacy of Man, the inventor of these blessing. Yet still they would intrigue against us, return us evil for good. And their inconsistency! To lie is what they term a sin; yet they make no scruple of lying when it comes to sneaking in among us on their treasonable missions, with forged basic ration books and identity cards. Of course they can always satisfy their consciences, I suppose, by obtaining a licence to commit sin from their priests in the confessional."

He paused for laughter.

"Look for a moment at the story they prize most, which lies at the very root of their religion. It is the story of a failure. Observe how they relish the grisly details of its end; they gloat upon the agony and bloody sweat, the mock crown, the brutal scourging, the thirst, the nakedness, the wounds. In a word, they worship Pain personified. You may think that this in itself renders their belief harmless; what sane man could subscribe to a religion which glorifies pain? And yet, whether it is that there is a seed of masochism in Man, or whether, still struggling out of adolescence, he has not yet shaken off the romanticism inherent in youth, the fact remains that this evil nonsense may fascinate him, may tempt him. He is, if I may so put it, like one who has just learnt to swim, and in deep waters screams suddenly for the lifebelt."

Sir Edward frowned. It was not, he realized, a very happy simile. There were still occasions when men drowned, and in drowning had every possible reason to scream for the lifebelt. This unreasonable weather, he decided, was responsible for such a gaffe.

"They come here, these Christians," he thundered, "accepting the State's hospitality, taking advantage of all the wonders of our technological age, on purpose to destroy us. Nor will there ever be wanting these mischievous, ill-disposed persons who, envious of our tranquillity and impatient of our triumphs, seek to challenge the supremacy of Man. If I may borrow a mataphor from one of their favourite myths, there is the serpent in our Eden. Mark how these enemies never dare to come openly to our shores; no! as has always been their jesuitical custom, they take false names, carry forged documents, dissemble their true purpose. Why, if it is innocent? I tell you, member of the jury, religion has always been the favourite mask for treason.

"But I thank Brotherhood that the prisoner has put us on our guard. My learned friend on the other side remarked that the accused had, though unwittingly, brought home once more to all men the malice of Christians. I for my part hope he has reawakened in us a wholesome fear of Christianity. Do not let us soothe away our fears with the obvious question, How could a handful of fanatics be right, and the whole of the civilized world be wrong? For the more wrong a man is, so much the more dangerous is he. The defence has asked you to show mercy, but mercy is mere weakness when the safety of the body politic is at stake. I ask you with confidence, to set an example to your fellow citizens, by showing your loyalty to Man in your verdict against the prisoner."

(ii)

The measured tones from the Bench were in striking contrast to the emotionalism displayed by counsel on both sides, as the Lord Chief Justice began his summing up. He might be a little past it, but his old-world dignity, his strict impartiality, lent tone to the proceedings.

Now and again the thunder interrupted him. Nature appeared to be in one of her worst moods; there had just been a shocking earthquake in the East, and a hurricane was devastating America's western seaboard. The Lord Chief Justice merely paused for the thunder to pass, as one might any rude interruption, and then resumed.

"Members of the jury, the charge against the prisoner is the gravest known to law. Even murder is as a trifling fault in comparison with this monstrous crime, for while homicide injures individuals, treason strikes at the State, and the State means those who are its citizens, it means ourselves. Yet this case, like all criminal cases, must be judged dispassionately; we must be careful to deal with it according to the evidence. Justice is ever in jeopardy when emotion is aroused."

He cast a gravely reproving glance at counsel, and then went deeply into the law of treason, which, said he, was of extreme interest. The law required that overt acts charged against the prisoner should be proved by two witnesses, either two to one overt act, or one witness to one and another witness to another overt act, both of the same treason. Overt acts, he was careful to explain, were such as manifest a criminal intention, and tended towards the accomplishment of the criminal object.

The teenagers among the jury began to fidget; why couldn't the old fuddie-duddie get on with it?

"In this case," continued the Lord Chief Justice, serenely unaware of such criticism, "the overt acts can be divided into two parts, the first dealing with the prisoner's coming from the Hebrides, contrary to the Reservations Act; the second with his activities between the period of his coming over and his very terrible attempt to hang himself at a Home of Rest. This attempt, though an offence, you must dismiss from your minds; counsel for the defence has told you, quite rightly, that it is irrelevant to the charge of treason. It is quite possible for you to come to the conclusion that both sets of overt acts were really part and parcel of the same scheme; that in coming to this country the prisoner's purpose was to solicit and incite the citizens to forsake their duty to the State, and transfer their allegiance to a mythical Being. I must remind you, however, that it is not necessary for you to find that all the overt acts are proved. One overt act properly proved is all that is sufficient to constitute treason."

He went carefully and minutely through the evidence, and resumed:

"The defence has told you that it is difficult, almost impossible, for you to divine what passes in the mind of a Christian. But a man's intentions are to be gathered from his acts. When an intelligent man does an act which would appear reasonably to involve certain consequences, then you are entitled to assume that he intended those consequences.

"I have already said to you all that I think necessary to say upon the law. I will conclude only by impressing upon you that if you have a reasonable doubt in the matter after considering the evidence, it is your duty to acquit the prisoner. But if, after viewing all the facts and circumstances, the conviction is borne in upon you that the prisoner has committed the offence with which he is charged, then it is your duty to return a verdict to that effect, and to take no regard of the consequences which must follow.

"You will now retire and consider your verdict."

They won't be long, thought the Lord Chief justice, sinking into his favourite armchair. Juries made what were called snap decisions nowadays, a habit he deplored.

He felt exceedingly indignant with the witness, Stephen Coles. So flippant and cynical. He must find out which Animals' Holiday Camp the man was at; it was awful to think that he, the Lord Chief Justice, might inadvertently send his Tiggles there this summer. On the other hand he had been very much affected by Mrs Jane Smith; she reminded him of a kindly old maiden aunt of his, who had treated some childish ailment he had contracted with a herbal medicine – fortunately the doctor had arrived in time with his hypodermic.

Mr Justice Fraser was worrying over his sixth wife who, at breakfast that morning, had announced her intention of applying to the Ministry of Divorce. "It's just that you're too old, pet; you've had it." She was right, of course, that was what worried him. His memory was failing. Try as he would, he could not remember the name of his first wife. Margery, he thought, but she might have been his second.

Mr Justice Caldicot, on the other hand, munching pep-chocolate, was practising the wriggle-whine, the very latest dance hit, in front of his portable television set, somewhat hampered by his robes.

Caldicot is right, thought the two elder men, watching with distaste that gentleman's wrigglings of his behind; one simply had to be "with it"; but each of them was filled with nostalgia for a simpler, kindlier past. They detested the slang used by the witnesses, the smoking in Court, the transistors turned on almost before they had left the Bench. They dared not say so, of course; to be out of touch with contemporary thought meant the end of one's career. It is true, thought the Lord Chief Justice, that we have abolished sin, and poverty, and war; but somehow or other, self-sacrifice, chivalry, and compassion seem to have disappeared along with these evils.

(iii)

The jury were out half an hour. They asked for certain Exhibits; not, indeed, to assist them in making up their minds, but out of frank curiosity. These grotesque toys of the prisoner; was it possible that an educated Englishman in this technological age could attach any importance to a string of beads, a coloured thread, a book of gibberish in antiquated language? Worst of all to the image of a Man enduring the most brutal and humiliating death?

"Are you agreed upon your verdict?" demanded the State's Coroner, when they had answered to their names.

"Yep," replied the forewoman tersely.

"How say you; do you find the prisoner, Peter Simon Diplock, guilty or not guilty of the high treason whereof he stands indicted?"

"Guilty."

The verdict caused no sensation, for everyone had known what it would be. But spectators craned and rustled, for a rumour had got around that the prisoner intended to make a speech.

"Peter Simon Diplock," said the State's Coroner, "you sand convicted of high treason. What have you to say for yourself why the Court should not pass sentence and judgement upon you according to law?"

Every eye was upon the man in the dock, and an enormous silence fell, as profound as the hush of death. He was a curiously timeless figure, his beard grown, a muffler round his neck in place of collar and tie, his shapeless old coat falling loose about him. It was obvious that he was nervous and overwrought, but he no longer cringed, and when he began to speak there was a note of desperate sincerity in his voice which impressed the spectators. Several noticed how often his eyes strayed with a wistful look towards the Exhibits on the table.

"First, I must make an objection, possibly not good in law, but surely good on moral grounds, against the application to me here of this old Statute of Treason. When it was passed in 1352, England was Christian kingdom in a united Christendom; it was passed by those who all subscribed to the very doctrines for which I am condemned. An indictment of those days invariably included the words, 'not having the fear of God before his eyes, but being seduced by the instigation of the Devil'. The law under which I am charged takes for granted the allegiance of all men to Almighty God, the Ruler of the world, supreme above all earthy powers; and it takes for granted also the existence of positive evil. You have abolished," he said, with the ghost of a smile, "the very language in which that statute was written; Latin is outlawed because it is the tongue of the Universal Church. I ask you, is it rational to use a Christian statute to try and to condemn a man only for being a Christian? Would those who made that law condemn me? Therefore they shall be your judges."

The Attorney General glanced sharply at the Bench. The prisoner should be stopped, since it was clear that he could not make any legal objection to the sentence. Possibly this might have given the impression that the Court was afraid of what he might say; but Sir Edward strongly suspected that both the elder judges were secretly curious, even vaguely sympathetic.

"I must correct two statements made by the Attorney General," went on Peter. "First that Christians insist that God sent suffering into the world; on the contrary, we insist that it was man who, by his disobedience to his Creator, brought suffering into the perfect world God made. Secondly the prosecution stated that Christian missionaries desire to stir up civil strife and rebellion. That is an abominable falsehood. The same charge was brought against Our Lord Jesus Christ, who replied that His kingdom was not of this world: treason has always been the excuse when men have persecuted Christians. There was a further misstatement which I must correct; that I accepted, under false pretences, the material benefits of the State, In fact, until my – my betrayal of my Master, I subsisted upon the alms of friends and sympathizers, and though I must not name them here, I take this opportunity of expressing my gratitude for their charity. As for my coming here in disguise, that is not exclusive to Christians; any man seeking to enter a country which regards him as its enemy, must perforce come in secret, however innocent his purpose."

He straightened his shoulders and gripped the rail of the dock, as though bracing himself for an ordeal.

"I must speak now of my guilt. The learned judge has said that my attempt to take my own life at Fremley Manor is irrelevant to the charge of treason. With great respect, I beg to differ. 'Suicide,' said St Thomas Aquinas, 'is the most fatal of sins, because it cannot be repented of.' Throughout her history, the Christian Church has taught that our life is given to us by God, and that its duration on earth is in His hands. I committed, in intention, the most deadly of all forms of high treason against my Maker; in despair of His mercy, I endeavoured to deface His image in myself. Of that, indeed, I am guilty; and while I must dispute your jurisdiction, as pagans, to condemn a Christian under a Christian statute, I submit myself wholly to the judgement of God, against whom I have most grievously sinned."

His eyes searched the crowded court-room, and rested for a moment on one figure in it.

"There is a lady, the principal witness against me, to whom I would like to express, publicly, my eternal gratitude. Had she not prevented me, I should have died, as Judas Iscariot died, in despair, Had she not shamed me into admitting it, I might have denied, even here in this Court, that ever I came from the Hebrides. But now I thank God I do not deny it; I did come from the Hebrides, and I came for the purpose of teaching the truths of the Christian religion.

"And now I must say a word in defence of that religion, which I betrayed. Somewhere in his speech, the Attorney General asked if it were conceivable that a handful of fanatics could be right, and the whole of the civilized world could be wrong. But *I* ask you, is it not at least remarkable that after two thousand years the Christian cause, persecuted by unbelievers throughout the world, and all down the ages, yet survives? And survives in spite of those sorry Christians who, like myself, have succumbed to the surrounding paganism? Does that not make you wonder whether, after all, it is more than human, whether there is something greater than what you call Humanity?

"If so, you may ask, why has it not triumphed? Why has it always been persecuted? I can answer you only that persecution is what Christ Our Lord foretold. 'Ye shall be hated of all men for My name's sake', and again, 'Blessed shall you be when men shall hate you, and when they shall separate you, and reproach you, and cast out your name as evil, for the Son of Man's sake'. Generation after generation has suffered for that sake; but each generation renews the claims of the last. If we are to be indicted as criminals and imprisoned as convicts because we obey the commandments of God and love Him more than we value our lives and reputations, that is only what our Master prophesied. The Cross is still the sign of contradiction, and will be to the end of the world."

All his nervousness had left him now. His eyes burned in his bearded face, and his voice vibrated with passion.

"But it is also the sign of our salvation. Reject it, and thought you may achieve a material utopia, you will have empty hearts; though you may have peace among nations, you will find no peace in your own souls. It is the banner of the noblest cause for which a man can live or die; and had I lived worthily for it, I should be proud indeed to be called a traitor; were I condemned to die for it, I should die in a right noble company of saints and martyrs. Sentence me, indeed, and you will be the instruments of God's justice against my sin; but do not sentence unheard the cause I betrayed, do not revile as enemies those who, knowing full well what they risk, come here from the reservations, and will continue to come here from the reservations, not to war against your State, but to tell you of another State, an eternal State, which is your true home."

The Attorney General made an audible aside at this point; a mercy bomb, he murmured, would speedily put an end to these invasions. Peter looked full at him, and smiled; it was a childish smile, almost sly.

"Oh no," he said softly. "That is the mistake all the enemies of Christianity have made throughout the centuries. It is absurd, they said, and therefore it will die a natural death; but it lived on, and so they crucufied it. But it rose again, and always will. For the Gates of Hell shall not prevail against it; nor can it fail; nor will it fail.

"My lord, I have done. Members of the jury, I thank you for your verdict."

"Peter Simon Diplock," said the Lord Chief Justice, "you have been found guilty of high treason, the gravest crime known to the law, and upon evidence which in our opinion is conclusive of guilt. The duty now devolves on me of passing sentence upon you, and it is that you be taken hence to a Reformation Camp, there to remain for the term of your natural life."

Chapter Five

(i)

This is where I came in, thought Clare, taking her seat in a chromium, plastic-covered chair with foam cushions, before the Board of Investigation. This is how it all began. It was not, of course, the same Board who had heard her application to self-eliminate; but it was going to decide her future just as the other had done.

Ever since the trial of Peter Diplock, she had become again the plaything of the Mental Health authorities. She was watched, observed, probed, her every reaction noted, everything she said and did written down and added up like a sum. But the conclusions they were coming to no longer mattered to her; she was too deeply immersed in her own mental gropings. During her daily visit to the psychiatrist, she had talked not so much to him as to herself, thinking aloud, caring very little for his busy note-taking.

This particular psychiatrist was an up-to-the-minute progressive, a leading member of the Friends of the Body who preached the cause of Nudity. There were frequent clashes between them and various trade unions whose members were concerned with the manufacture of clothes. Meanwhile, until his cause received the sanction of law, this psychiatrist did his best, going about, summer and winter, in singlet and shorts, exposing skinny bare limbs. The neatly furled umbrella hooked to his arm struck an odd note. He pranced about his consulting-room smoking a reefer; he was a skittish man.

The Mental Health authorities were concerned for her, he told Clare, in case she might have caught a naughty little bug from the nonsense talked to her at Fremley by the man named Peter. The psychiatrist explained carefully, as to a child, that "God" was merely the terrifying vengeful father-image of Jewish conception, the horde-father of Freud. "Christ," on the other hand, was the creation of the Unconscious to compensate for that image, a creation dominated by love and tenderness.

"It's as simple as that," said he, "so not to worry."

"It seems to me," she said mildly, "infinitely more complicated than the Christian doctrine."

He ignored this, and continued, warming to his subject:

"It's fascinating to see how much Christianity has in common with the Totemism of primitive peoples. There is the cannibal feast they call Communion, in which they devour their Victim and so acquire part of his strength. And then there's jolly old Original Sin, which is nothing, of course, but a primal guilt-complex surviving through thousands of years. There's the observance of Taboo, which they call 'conscience', with a belief in sprites and demons. There's the illusion which is the prime condition of all group-life, the illusion on the part of the members that they are loved by their leader. Actually, pet, the sense of guilt engendered by the incestuous desires of the dear old Oedipus-complex is the innate foundation of all religion. Man the Scientist has hoist God with his own petard by showing that religion carries all the marks of a child-mentality – "

" 'Unless you become as little children, you cannot enter the Kingdom of Heaven.' "

"You've got it in one, pet. Religion derives its strength from the fact that it panders to our instinctual desires."

"And might they not be real? As real as tables and chairs," she added, suddenly remembering Linda saying that.

"Oh, come off it, poppet! Religion is the product of imagination, having nothing to do with reality."

"That's what you say, without giving any grounds for it. You simply make statements, general assumptions, Except for some sort of technical training, you've no more right to lay down the law about human nature than I have. And what about some of the most powerful intellects the human race has ever produced? They didn't think that religion was illusory. The fact that you do, doesn't make it so."

He was not in the least offended; he was used to such outbursts from his patients. He simply began all over again about the dear old Libido and the jolly little Id.

"Now tell us, dear Clare," said the President of the Board of Investigation, "what you yourself would like to do."

"I think I would very much like to go to a Home of Rest again; one part of me would, at least. But another part wouldn't, so I shan't apply."

They nodded wisely.

"I suppose, if I made application, I could go to the Hebrides?"

"Oh certainly."

"Which would probably come to the same thing in the end; I mean, if this mercy bomb idea gets passed by the World Parliament. To die in such company might be easier – "

"I doubt that, you know. There will be panic there – "

"Oh, do you think so? I don't myself."

"Undoubtedly there will be," said the President, rather huffed. Who was she to express opinions? "Whereas in our Homes of Rest, the martyrs are prepared for euthanasia. Two healing weeks – "

"Drugs. You seem to forget I've been to one. But I can't apply to go to the Hebrides; it wouldn't be honest."

"No, dear Clare," he murmured. "You cannot go back to being a savage."

She shook her head with impatience. She wished he would not be so omniscient, would stop putting words into her mouth.

"It isn't like that at all. It wouldn't be honest because I don't believe in what they believe in, and for which they may be going to be eliminated. I should be – an intruder, like the man who came to the feast without a wedding-garment."

They all smiled pityingly. She was quoting from the Christian Scriptures; she was like a mature person reading fairy-tales for the first time and actually wondering if they might be true. The President began a little homily on the marvellous inventions of Man, but she interrupted.

"Surely they're not inventions; merely discoveries. They were all there – electricity, nuclear power, even the new drugs and the ingredients of the mercy bomb. Man has simply discovered them, and can use them or abuse them. And there's one thing you've neither invented nor discovered – the creation of life. You take people and break them up into little bits, like a butcher carving up a carcase. This bit fits here, you say, and that bit there; and it all adds up like a sum. But you're not even sure you've got the bits in place. You didn't make them, so how can you – be sure, I mean? It's easy enough to pull a flower to pieces; can you put it together again? You can't even create a fly."

209

"One day we shall. It is the last secret. Throughout the ages men have devoted themselves to discover the secret of Life. And now, with all the resources of contemporary Science – "

"Suppose you did discover it? Who would control it? Some abstraction called the State, which already sterilizes the unfit and eliminates the insane? Would it also wield this unimaginable power of creating, or refusing to create, life itself?" Something in the President's expression made her cry: "Or would it be a person, like as it might be yourself? 'I will be like God'. I don't know where I've heard or read that, but wasn't it the sin of the angels in the Christian story? 'I will be equal with God.' I suppose it was an allegory; I don't know what the Christians say. But what it means surely is – well, rebellion, the ultimate rebellion, some act of pride so unforgivable that Hell was the only answer. All right! But even Man has found that pride is dangerous. Wasn't it a prime cause of war?"

Someone on the Board begged her to be calm and reasonable. She really must make an effort to adjust herself, to fit into contemporary thought-forms.

"Like a bit of a jigsaw puzzle," said Clare. "But if there is a jigsaw, then someone must have created it, have thought it out. Not Man; not even his most fervent devotees claim Creation for him, only Evolution. And you appeal to my reason, always and only to my reason, as though there weren't other parts of me which might be equally important. It's like you picking out a few texts from the Scriptures and ditching the rest. But any man, or at least any woman, could tell you that the heart is as essential a part of us as the intellect. And the heart must suffer; I don't know why, and you don't know why, but that's how it seems to have been created. If it doesn't suffer, it doesn't love, and if it doesn't love it withers."

"I am afraid the trouble with you, dear Clare, put into simple language," said the President gently, "is that you have a reactionary fixation. You secretly yearn to put the clock back."

"Well why not, if the clock has gone wrong?"

"Contemporary clocks *can't* go wrong," he told her with smiling complacence.

"I sometimes wonder," remarked Clare dryly, "whether Man hasn't got a Narcissus-complex, or fixation, or whatever you call it. If he could only look away from himself to something higher, he might find himself."

"Man will only be fully mature when there is a common agreement between us psychologists. I dream of the day when the Functionalists, the Mentalists, the Behaviourists, and the Structuralists agree on an exact definition of Mind." He glanced at his watch. "And now, if you would leave us for a little while, we will debate your case."

(ii)

I retire while they consider their verdict, she thought, while they reduce me, a human being, to phrases from a text-book, to a complicated sum which they work out in fractions.

She wandered to the window and stood looking out, down on to the perfectly controlled traffic on the soundless rubber streets, upwards to the gigantic blocks of flats and offices which reared like new Towers of Babel into the smokeless air, pointing towards the sky which seemed to be permanently overcast, as though Heaven had been closed against man. Whatever they to do with me, she thought, I'll have to find myself; and she remembered what Stephen had said, it seemed in another life, that her job was not to give herself up.

211

For the first time for months Michael jumped into her mind; and now, amazingly, grudgingly, she saw his "thing" about Barbara as gallant and right. I suppose, she told herself, that it's because I'll probably be sent to a Mental Home, and oh if only there were going to someone waiting for me when I come out again, someone unreasonable enough to stick by me even though I wasn't any use to them. But only the god-almighty State will be waiting, to put me back on the conveyor-belt, to move me about like a pawn on a chessboard, to give me everything that it considers makes life worth living – except happiness and peace of mind.

We've got our values all wrong somehow, she thought desperately, thumping her fists against the plastic window-frame. I know it as certainly as I used to know when a drawing was wrong, out of focus, lacking a central point. And often and often I just had to tear it up, and begin all over again. How effortless your drawing is, Miss Bentley, people used to say, people who knew nothing about the agony, the blood and sweat and tears that go with creation. You can't create without pain.

Pain! How it came back, that "dirty" word, how it forced itself upon her consciousness, making her see, against her will, against all the modern attitudes, that it was essential to the mysterious scheme of life. Neither art nor love nor friendship could be complete without it; it was like salt; if it lost its savour, the dish became insipid. Nor could Man abolish it, no, not with all his mercy drugs, his material security, his free this and free that; he had to acknowledge that crime and mental illness were on the increase, that as fast as he conquered one disease, Nature faced him with another; and that even though he triumphed over all the ills of the body, the human heart defied him to give it peace or satisfaction. How else explain the fact that more and more citizens of this new utopia were seeking the last desperate remedy, euthanasia, were clamouring for admission to the Home of Rest?

Is it, I wonder, can it possibly be, that we are not meant to find satisfaction here? That quotation Stephen so surprisingly brought out in the witness-box – "Thou hast made us for Thyself". That would explain a lot of problems; it might even be the only explanation, fantastic though it sounds.

Very well, then; supposing for a moment that it is; the question follows, Can *I* accept it? Can I range myself on the side of the cranks, I who always prided myself on being so forward-looking, who was so impatient with poor Linda (or perhaps, lucky Linda) who went to the Hebrides because she had to find out whether God existed or not? I thought then, I even suspect now, that she was simply running away from life in a crisis; but then, to be honest, so did I, in another way, very shortly afterwards. What she did was harder than what I did; she went to the reservations to face life in the raw, life on all its planes; a sort of pioneer. I went to a Home of Rest to be prepared by a fortnight of drugs and pep talks for a gentle and easy death...

"Gutless," "Cowards' Hall" – oh damn Stephen. I hated him at Fremley; and then at the trial I rather admired him. I wonder what he's doing now.

Then she remembered with a pang that wherever Stephen was, he had Dragon. It was on Stephen that Dragon now lavished those wet kisses, for him that there sounded the scrabble of long-nailed feet, that ecstatic whine; on Stephen's bed that warm soft body now lay, with hind paws and tail protruding in an abandoned posture. Dragon had snarled at her as though she had snarled at her as though she had betrayed him when she had taken him into the Temple of Rest...

No, not on Stephen's bed. In a kennel, more likely. "He's very happy learning to be a dog." Dog-nature, human-nature, each created differently; the instinct of an animal, the reason of a man; can both be abused? If so, that argues a Creator who has set limits and laid down laws. And we can't possibly know what those laws are unless we acknowledge the Creator. And I can't acknowledge Him – why? Is it just possible that there's something lacking that I can't supply? Something the Christians call faith, which, as I understand it from their Gospels, is a gift which has to be asked for? I might be too small for it; on the other hand I might be too big. Like Alice when she found the golden key, but couldn't get even her head through the tiny doorway. Perhaps if I found a little bottle on the table marked FAITH… what awful bloody nonsense I'm talking.

Something Peter had said recurred to her, something about his having deliberately cut off communications with God. But surely, she thought, prayer must always be like speaking into a dead telephone; nobody answers. She had a sudden vivid mental picture of herself as a small child in a nightgown, kneeling beside her bed and repeating a little prayer. She could only remember one line of it now, "Pity my simplicity," and that because for years she had thought it was, "Pity mice in plicity"; "plicity" must be some disease peculiar to mice, she had supposed, and was pleased and surprised that one could pray for dumb creatures.

"But if You existed, God," she said, not knowing that she spoke aloud, "that's just what I would ask You for – pity. Because if You existed that's what You'd feel; pity for Your poor, troubled Creation, men and women, dogs and mice… "

She broke off. A most curious sensation had fallen on her, making her spine tingle. It was as though, speaking into a dead telephone, she had caught, very, very faintly, a kind of vibration, as of some Presence at the other end.

"Well, my dear Clare," said the President of the Board, "we have reached our conclusion."

They had been a very long time reaching it, not because her case was complicated, but because they had been indulging in academic hate, aroused by the President's last remark before Clare left them. Two of them had nearly come to blows over an exact definition of Mind.

"I am very glad indeed to tell you that there is nothing worse than a little temporary mental derangement. You have a schizoid reaction, which means a fragmentation of the personality. A review of your life history has revealed that you showed signs of this even in childhood; you have always been solitary and over-imaginative. Part of your trouble is a not uncommon one in persons of your generation. You were just too old to have been trained by psychoanalysts during the first four vital years of your life, when repressions, complexes and inhibitions must be dealt with in order to secure future psychic orientation. Instead, you were under the care of ignorant parents – ignorant, that is, of the method of applying the Pleasure Principle to the aims of advanced Science. This set up a complex in which you dreaded, yet at the same time rejoiced in, Authority. Over-late emancipation," he continued darkly, "has caused Stagnation and Regression to appear. Even up to the age of fourteen you lacked an Analyst-Educator, and you know what Pfister says in his work, *The Psycho-Analytic Method*, on the dangers of the old forms of education. Why, you must have been far advanced in adolescence before you were taught to make use of the Subconscious. A later symptom is your lack of interest in a thing and also in a person formerly of the greatest possible attraction to you. Our recent talks have revealed that your mind has become a jumble of ideas without coherence, and that you are a prey to dangerous delusions. The next stage might well be the illusion of hearing voices talking to you, like the classic case of schizophrenia, Joan of Arc."

He lifted a deprecating hand, and added:

"But modern treatment, I can assure you, will arrest the progress of the disease, and effect, we hope, a permanent cure. This treatment is aimed at pricking you into contact with Reality, and persuading you to abandon your phantasy life."

He closed the huge case-book with finality.

"You will find this Mental Home a most congenial place. It is in the country, so quiet and peaceful; a kind of temporary Home of Rest," he added with a kindly smile.

(iii)

Stephen parked the estate-car in the station yard of Terminus Five. Switching off the engine, he said over his shoulder to the wagonload of dogs he was taking to the Animals' Holiday Camp:

"Afraid you're going to miss Puppies' Hour on TV, boys and girls; might even miss this week's episode of 'Venus, the Bitch Detective'. But it can't be helped." He thought of the White Coats waiting to show the guests to their chalet-pens, to distract their attention from the inoculations with chocolate-flavoured bones. I'm going to lose this job very shortly, he thought, and then what the Hebrides am I going to do next? "Dragon," he said abruptly, "you stay here. I'd like to take you on to the platform, but it wouldn't be fair to you or her."

He saw Clare immediately he got on to the platform, some minutes before she saw him. She was in the train, framed in an open window, looking out. He had expected to find her miserable, even distracted; but instead, her face wore a strange, rapt expression, as of one immersed in a

216

problem of the deepest interest. She looked younger than at Fremley, almost child-like; she could have been a little girl going off to school, to a new school, nervous but at the same time excited. When he spoke to her, she looked at him with eyes unfocused; behind her in the carriage he could see her new custodian, presumably a nurse though she wore no uniform, a bright, mechanically tactful young person, a sort of female Mr Reddington.

"Dragon's here somewhere," remarked Clare evenly. "I know his bark; just like an alsatian's."

"And who's that dragon behind you, sitting in the corner pretending to read?"

"She's someone from the Mental Home who's been sent to fetch me. But she's not pretending to read; she's absolutely absorbed in a paperback called *Star of the West.* It's all about an American girl who got separated from a wagon train and captured by Indians. She and the Chief's son are just about to fall in love, but she thinks her beau is looking for her, whereas the reader knows that far from being the clean American type she thinks he is, he's fallen for a singer in a low sa-loon."

"Would you please stop telling rather silly lies?"

"I'm not. Everyone has to have escapism. I do so wonder what the psychologists read when they're off-duty. In fact I wonder about them, full stop. Do little psychologists have bigger psychologists upon their backs to analyse 'em? Who takes care of the psycho's psyche where the psycho's busy taking care– "

"Clare, will you stop it? I came to say something, and I bloody well won't be sidetracked. The whole thing's absolutely damnable. They've bamboozled you, pushed you around, ever since Fremley. They've just used you, and now that you've served your purpose as a witness against the wretched Peter, they're disposing of you like – like – "

"Oh no, no, no!" she interrupted, in a little silvery voice that seemed to have a bubble of laughter in it. "It isn't like that at all. *They* haven't disposed of me."

"Then who has?"

"I don't know." She looked away from him, suddenly shy. "But it doesn't matter where I am, I've got to find myself, and I can do that in a Mental Home just as well as anywhere else. The law of diminishing returns is operating; I've grown at least semi-immune to the effects of their psychology already."

The train began faintly to hum, preparatory to gliding away from the platform. He wanted most desperately to snatch her out.

"I've stopped running away from whatever is chasing me," she said without coherence. "If there *is* anything, it will have to catch me up. Or you can put it that I've got to go along a road all on my own, until I come to a sign which says, HALT. MAJOR ROAD AHEAD."

"And then what?"

"I haven't the least idea. Only there will be a signpost. As for the psychos, I've passed them. Did you ever meet a herd of cows while you were driving? Tiresome, and delaying, but going about their cowly business, and really quite harmless."

The train started to move.

"Clare, I came to tell you that Dragon and I will be waiting for you when you come out. Don't care how long it is, we'll be on the doorstep. Or just Dragon, if you'd rather; you always found me such a bloody boor."

He was running along the platform now, trying to keep pace with the quickening train.

"Clare, I'm sorry I said you were gutless at Fremley; you're just about the most gallant creature I've ever met."

She looked back at him; and her eyes were wet. Michael waiting for Barbara; the wheel had turned full circle.

"Oh, go to the Hebrides!" she cried, half laughing, and half weeping. But it was a prayer, and not an imprecation.

JANE LANE

A CALL OF TRUMPETS

Civil war rages in England, rendering it a minefield of corruption and conflict. Town and country are besieged. Through the complex interlocking of England's turmoil with that of a king, Jane Lane brings to life some amazing characters in the court of Charles I. This is the story both of Charles' adored wife whose indiscretions prove disastrous, and of the King's nephew, Rupert, a rash, arrogant soldier whose actions lead to tragedy and his uncle's final downfall.

CONIES IN THE HAY

1586 was the year of an unbearably hot summer when treachery came to the fore. In this scintillating drama of betrayals, Jane Lane sketches the master of espionage, Francis Walsingham, in the bright, lurid colours of the deceit for which he was renowned. Anthony Babington and his fellow conspirators are also brought to life in this vivid, tense novel, which tells of how they were duped by Walsingham into betraying the ill-fated Mary, Queen of Scots, only to be hounded to their own awful destruction.

JANE LANE

HIS FIGHT IS OURS

His Fight Is Ours follows the traumatic trials of MacIain, a Highland Chieftain of the clan Donald, as he leads his people in the second Jacobite rising on behalf of James Stuart, the Old Pretender. The battle to restore the king to his rightful throne is portrayed here in this absorbing historical escapade, which highlights all the beauty and romance of Highland life. Jane Lane presents a dazzling, picaresque story of the problems facing MacIain as leader of a proud, ancient race, and his struggles against injustice and the violent infamy of oppression.

A SUMMER STORM

Conflict and destiny abound as King Richard II, a chivalrous, romantic and idealist monarch, courts his beloved Anne of Bohemia. In the background, the swirling rage of the Peasants' Revolt of 1381 threatens to topple London as the tides of farmers, labourers and charismatic rebel hearts flood the city. This tense, powerful historical romance leads the reader from bubbling discord to doomed love all at the turn of a page.

Jane Lane

Thunder on St Paul's Day

London is gripped by mass hysteria as Titus Oates uncovers the Popish Plot, and a gentle English family gets caught up in the terrors of trial and accusation when Oates points the finger of blame. The villainous Oates adds fuel to the fire of an angry mob with his sham plot, leaving innocence to face a bullying judge and an intimidated jury. Only one small boy may save the family in this moving tale of courage pitted against treachery.

A Wind Through the Heather

A Wind Through the Heather is a poignant, tragic story based on the Highland Clearances where thousands of farmers were driven from their homes by tyrannical and greedy landowners. Introducing the Macleods, Jane Lane recreates the shameful past suffered by an innocent family who lived to cross the Atlantic and find a new home. This wistful, historical novel focuses on the atrocities so many bravely faced and reveals how adversities were overcome.

OTHER TITLES BY JANE LANE AVAILABLE DIRECT
FROM HOUSE OF STRATUS

Quantity	£	$(US)	$(CAN)	€
BRIDGE OF SIGHS	6.99	12.95	16.95	11.50
A CALL OF TRUMPETS	6.99	12.95	16.95	11.50
CAT AMONG THE PIGEONS	6.99	12.95	16.95	11.50
COMMAND PERFORMANCE	6.99	12.95	16.95	11.50
CONIES IN THE HAY	6.99	12.95	16.95	11.50
COUNTESS AT WAR	6.99	12.95	16.95	11.50
THE CROWN FOR A LIE	6.99	12.95	16.95	11.50
DARK CONSPIRACY	6.99	12.95	16.95	11.50
EMBER IN THE ASHES	6.99	12.95	16.95	11.50
FAREWELL TO THE WHITE COCKADE	6.99	12.95	16.95	11.50
FORTRESS IN THE FORTH	6.99	12.95	16.95	11.50
HEIRS OF SQUIRE HARRY	6.99	12.95	16.95	11.50
HIS FIGHT IS OURS	6.99	12.95	16.95	11.50

ALL HOUSE OF STRATUS BOOKS ARE AVAILABLE FROM GOOD BOOKSHOPS
OR DIRECT FROM THE PUBLISHER:

Internet: www.houseofstratus.com including author interviews, reviews, features.

Email: sales@houseofstratus.com please quote author, title and credit card details.

OTHER TITLES BY JANE LANE AVAILABLE DIRECT
FROM HOUSE OF STRATUS

Quantity		£	$(US)	$(CAN)	€
	THE PHOENIX AND THE LAUREL	6.99	12.95	16.95	11.50
	PRELUDE TO KINGSHIP	6.99	12.95	16.95	11.50
	QUEEN OF THE CASTLE	6.99	12.95	16.95	11.50
	THE SEALED KNOT	6.99	12.95	16.95	11.50
	A SECRET CHRONICLE	6.99	12.95	16.95	11.50
	THE SEVERED CROWN	6.99	12.95	16.95	11.50
	SIR DEVIL-MAY-CARE	6.99	12.95	16.95	11.50
	SOW THE TEMPEST	6.99	12.95	16.95	11.50
	A SUMMER STORM	6.99	12.95	16.95	11.50
	THUNDER ON ST PAUL'S DAY	6.99	12.95	16.95	11.50
	A WIND THROUGH THE HEATHER	6.99	12.95	16.95	11.50
	THE YOUNG AND LONELY KING	6.99	12.95	16.95	11.50

ALL HOUSE OF STRATUS BOOKS ARE AVAILABLE FROM GOOD BOOKSHOPS
OR DIRECT FROM THE PUBLISHER:

Internet: www.houseofstratus.com including synopses and features.

Email: sales@houseofstratus.com please quote author, title and
credit card details.

Order Line: UK: 0800 169 1780,
USA: 1 800 509 9942
INTERNATIONAL: +44 (0) 20 7494 6400 (UK)
or
+01 212 218 7649
(please quote author, title, and credit card details.)

Send to: House of Stratus Sales Department   House of Stratus Inc.
24c Old Burlington Street   Suite 210
London   1270 Avenue of the Americas
W1X 1RL   New York • NY 10020
UK   USA

PAYMENT

Please tick currency you wish to use:

☐ £ (Sterling)   ☐ $ (US)   ☐ $ (CAN)   ☐ € (Euros)

Allow for shipping costs charged per order plus an amount per book as set out in the tables below:

CURRENCY/DESTINATION

	£(Sterling)	$(US)	$(CAN)	€(Euros)
Cost per order				
UK	1.50	2.25	3.50	2.50
Europe	3.00	4.50	6.75	5.00
North America	3.00	3.50	5.25	5.00
Rest of World	3.00	4.50	6.75	5.00
Additional cost per book				
UK	0.50	0.75	1.15	0.85
Europe	1.00	1.50	2.25	1.70
North America	1.00	1.00	1.50	1.70
Rest of World	1.50	2.25	3.50	3.00

PLEASE SEND CHEQUE OR INTERNATIONAL MONEY ORDER.
payable to: STRATUS HOLDINGS plc or HOUSE OF STRATUS INC. or card payment as indicated

STERLING EXAMPLE

Cost of book(s):..................... Example: 3 x books at £6.99 each: £20.97

Cost of order: .... Example: £1.50 (Delivery to UK address)

Additional cost per book:.............. Example: 3 x £0.50: £1.50

Order total including shipping:.......... Example: £23.97

VISA, MASTERCARD, SWITCH, AMEX:

☐ ☐ ☐ ☐ ☐ ☐ ☐ ☐ ☐ ☐ ☐ ☐ ☐ ☐ ☐ ☐ ☐ ☐

Issue number (Switch only):

☐ ☐ ☐

Start Date: **Expiry Date:**

☐ ☐ / ☐ ☐   ☐ ☐ / ☐ ☐

Signature: _____

NAME: _____

ADDRESS: _____

COUNTRY: _____

ZIP/POSTCODE: _____

Please allow 28 days for delivery. Despatch normally within 48 hours.

Prices subject to change without notice.
Please tick box if you do not wish to receive any additional information. ☐

House of Stratus publishes many other titles in this genre; please check our website (**www.houseofstratus.com**) for more details.